Rahul Iyengar

Enid Blyton

MYSTERY

FREE GIFTS FROM
THE ARMADA COLLECTORS' CLUB

Look out for these tokens in your favourite Armada series! All you need to do to receive a special FREE GIFT is collect 6 tokens in the same series and send them off to the address below with a postcard marked with your name and address including postcode. Start collecting today!

Send your tokens to:

Armada Collectors' Club
HarperCollins Children's Books,
77 - 85 Fulham Palace Road,
London, W6 8JB

Or if you live in New Zealand to:

Armada Collectors' Club
HarperCollins Publishers Ltd.
31 View Road, Glenfield,
PO Box 1, Auckland

THIS OFFER APPLIES TO RESIDENTS OF THE U.K., EIRE AND NEW ZEALAND ONLY.

1 TOKEN
GB

Enid Blyton

THE RING O' BELLS
MYSTERY

Armada
HarperCollins*Publishers*

First published in the UK in 1951 by
George Newnes
First published in Armada in 1967
This edition published in 1993

Armada is an imprint of
HarperCollins Children's Books
part of HarperCollins Publishers Ltd
77-85 Fulham Palace Road
Hammersmith, London W6 8JB

Printed and bound in Great Britain by
HarperCollins Book Manufacturing, Glasgow

Chapter One

They Couldn't Go Back To School

'I thought those three children were going off to school today,' said Mr Lynton. 'Why aren't they down punctually to breakfast?'

'Oh, Richard – isn't it *tiresome* – Snubby and Diana aren't well,' said Mrs Lynton. 'They've both got temperatures – and I can't send Roger back in case Snubby and Diana are going to have something infectious. The school would not take him back if so.'

'Good gracious!' said Mr Lynton, exasperated. 'After four long weeks of Easter holidays, when there has been nothing but noise and racing about, and that dog Loony under my feet all the time – now we get another two or three weeks of it, I suppose!'

'Oh, well, Richard, we can't help it if they fall ill,' said his wife. 'Snubby really *must* be feeling bad – he can't even eat a sausage for his breakfast, and you know how fond he is of them.'

'It won't hurt him to starve for a week,' said Mr Lynton hard-heartedly. 'I'm not wasting any pity on Snubby. I've never known anyone eat as he does. They can't make a penny profit on Snubby at school, I'll be bound!'

He gathered up his papers and went off to catch his train, looking rather gloomy. He had been looking forward to a little peace in the house, with the three children enjoying themselves away at school. Now it looked as if they wouldn't be gone for another week or so, possibly longer.

Mrs Lynton went up to see Snubby. He groaned when

she came in. 'I do feel bad, Aunt Susan. And do you think you could possibly take Loony out again? He keeps wanting me to play and I can't bear it. He's such a very *scrapey* dog this morning – scrapes the clothes off me, and scrapes the rugs off the floor, and–'

'I know, I know,' said his aunt soothingly, pulling the clothes straight. 'There's not much about Loony that I don't know already. Now try to get a little sleep till the doctor comes. I'm going in to see Diana.'

Diana was feeling bad too. Mrs Lynton felt her hot hands. 'I think you've both got a touch of 'flu,' she said. 'What a pity, just at the end of the holidays!'

Roger still seemed all right, though he was in bed too, as he had just a slight temperature. He had been able to manage a little breakfast.

The doctor came at half-past ten, and tripped over Sardine, the cat, on the stairs. 'I'm so sorry,' said Mrs Lynton. 'I should have warned you! Sardine, if you do that again, I'll send Loony after you.'

'Dear me – who's Loony?' asked the doctor, and knew immediately, as Loony came racing down the stairs after Sardine, nearly sending him to the bottom.

He was a nice, cheery doctor, and the children liked him, though Snubby and Diana could only raise rather feeble smiles when he made his jokes.

'Ha! I suppose this is all faked just to get out of going back to school!' he said, taking Diana's hand to feel her pulse. 'I know these tricks! I've half a mind to order you up and about!'

'I couldn't possibly get up,' said Diana weakly. 'I got up in the night to get a drink and I could hardly stand.'

'Well, don't worry,' said the doctor cheerily. 'You've only got a touch of this wretched 'flu that's going round. You'll soon be all right.'

'Well, thank goodness it's only 'flu and not scarlet fever

or anything like that,' said Mrs Lynton, when the doctor went downstairs with her again.

'It's a pretty nasty 'flu, though,' said the doctor, looking for his gloves. 'Now – where did I put my gloves?'

'Loony! *You've* got them!' said Mrs Lynton sharply to the black spaniel. 'Drop them! Bad dog!'

The doctor got back his gloves at last. 'Well, as I was saying,' he said, 'it's a pretty nasty 'flu. Keep them in bed till I say they can get up – and then, I'm afraid, they ought not to go back to school for another ten days or so. They'll feel pretty washed out afterwards. Perhaps you could get them away somewhere.'

'I'll see what I can do,' said Mrs Lynton. 'Well, thank you, Doctor, I'll be seeing you tomorrow then.'

Roger was soon as bad as the others, and the amount of grumbling and groaning that went on was terrific. Perhaps the most miserable person in the house was Loony the spaniel. He wasn't ill, of course – but he simply couldn't understand why the three children were kept in bed and didn't appear to want his company at all!

'He's awful,' complained Diana. 'If I let him in, he goes mad, and I simply can't stand it, I've got such a headache – and if I don't let him in, he scrapes at the door and whines till I do. Can't Snubby have him in his room? He's Snubby's dog.'

'He doesn't want him either,' said Mrs Lynton. 'I'll send him out for a long walk with the baker's boy this afternoon. He's very fond of him, and would love to take him for a walk.'

'I don't mind Sardine so much,' said Diana. 'She doesn't stamp about like Loony. But I don't like it when she sits on my tummy and kneads me carefully with her claws as if I were a bit of dough. Oh, Mummy – I do feel bad!'

'Poor old girl,' said her mother. 'You'll soon feel all right again. Don't worry!'

Mrs Lynton had put Roger in a room by himself when Snubby had fallen ill, hoping that perhaps he wouldn't catch it. But now that it was certain he was in for the 'flu as well, she moved him back into his own room with his cousin Snubby. They both felt so miserable that she was sure they wouldn't get up to any tricks together just yet!

The illness ran its course, and in a few days all three were feeling decidedly better. 'If only my *legs* weren't so wobbly!' said Snubby. 'They feel as if they were made of jelly. Will they ever get all right again, Aunt Susan?'

'Of course. Don't be silly,' said his aunt. 'Anyway, *I* know you're much better because you asked for a sausage for breakfast this morning. Tomorrow you'll probably ask for three.'

'Woof,' said Loony, who always knew the word 'sausage' when he heard it. He put a big black paw on Snubby's bed, and looked mournfully at his master. He hadn't understood Snubby at all for the last few days. Snubby hadn't been pleased to see him – he hadn't yelled and laughed as usual – he hadn't even been pleased when Loony brought him a half-chewed and very smelly bone.

Snubby patted Loony's smooth, silky head, and fondled the black, drooping ears. 'I'm feeling better now, Loony,' he said. 'We'll soon be out for walkies again.'

'Woof!' said Loony excitedly, and leapt with one bound on to Snubby's middle. But that was more than Snubby could stand, and soon Loony was being taken sternly out of the room by Mrs Lynton.

'I think the children had better go away for a change of air,' Mrs Lynton said to her husband that night. 'They are all much better, but I feel rather tired myself now. I could get Miss Pepper, my old governess, to look after them for a bit, I know. She's very fond of them all.'

8

'Good idea,' said Mr Lynton warmly. 'I know what Snubby was like after he'd had a chill once – do you remember? He appeared to be twice as full of beans, and three times as full of cheek. I don't feel I could stand that after four or five weeks of him here.'

'Yes – that was the time when he managed to get up on the roof, wasn't it – and emptied a can of water down the dining-room chimney,' said Mrs Lynton. 'I remember how startled I was. Well – I think I'll ring up Miss Pepper and see what she thinks about it. She's very good at handling the three. She doesn't stand any nonsense.'

Miss Pepper said yes – she would take the three children off Mrs Lynton's hands with pleasure. It was a long time since she had seen them – not since they had all stayed at Rockingdown with her, and plunged into peculiar adventures!

'You'll see that they don't get up to mischief at all, won't you?' said Mrs Lynton anxiously. 'You know what they are – so headstrong and lively and daring. They want firm handling.'

'You needn't worry,' said Miss Pepper. 'Now where did you think of sending them? By the sea?'

'Well, no,' said Mrs Lynton. 'The doctor says some-where inland, but not too low – and somewhere fairly warm. He doesn't want them paddling or bathing or doing anything like that just yet. Can you suggest anywhere?'

There was a pause. Then Miss Pepper spoke doubtfully. 'Well – I do know a place. It's got a lovely name but it's not as pretty a village as it sounds. Have you heard of Ring O'Bells Village?'

'Yes – isn't it that very old place, near the town of Lillinghame?' said Mrs Lynton.

'That's right,' said Miss Pepper. 'I've a cousin who keeps a little boarding house there – I'm sure she would be pleased to have the children.'

They talked about the idea for a little while. Ring O' Bells sounded just right to Mrs Lynton. There were riding stables nearby, where the three children could hire horses and hack round the countryside. There were walks up the hills and through the woods. Miss Pepper was sure the air would do them good.

'Right,' said Mrs Lynton, thankful to have settled everything so easily. 'Will you telephone your cousin, Miss Pepper, and arrange everything? The children can travel this week, the doctor says – so I could pack them in the car, and drive over to you – and then drive down to Ring O' Bells. It really is a lovely name, and sounds so *peace*ful somehow.'

'Yes,' said Miss Pepper, wondering if it would be quite so peaceful when Loony and the three children got down there. Thank goodness there wouldn't be that strange circus friend of theirs there too – the boy Barney and his monkey, Miranda!

Chapter Two

Ring O' Bells Village

'Ring O' Bells Village!' said Diana delightedly, when she heard the news. 'Oh, mother – it sounds lovely. I should like to go there. It sounds as if it's out of a nursery rhyme.'

'Are there bells or something?' demanded Snubby, who was now up and looking more himself, though he was very pale under his thatch of red hair. Even his mass of freckles seemed to have faded. 'I'd like to ring church bells – you know, pull those ropes and make them play a tune.'

'It's not as easy as all that,' said his aunt. 'Well, I'm glad you are all pleased. You'll be able to ride, anyway, and you all like that. I believe Ring O' Bells is an interesting old village, too, with all kinds of stories and legends about it.'

'Good!' said Roger. 'I like places like that. You never know when you might find out about something mysterious.'

'I don't want you to go smelling out any mysteries or anything,' said his mother. 'I just want you to get well enough to go back to school as quickly as possible, so as not to miss any more of the lovely summer term than you need.'

School didn't appeal to the children very much just then. 'I believe I'd faint if I had to go and sit in a maths class now, Aunt Susan,' said Snubby, trying to sound pathetic. He had enjoyed being fussed over by his aunt.

He had no parents, and his Aunt Susan was the nearest he had known to a mother.

'It's much more likely that your maths master would faint,' said his aunt unsympathetically. 'He's probably thanking his stars that he hasn't had to cope with you yet this term, Snubby.'

'I'm afraid I shan't get much of a report this term, Aunt Susan,' said Snubby, still looking pathetic. 'I mean – if I get a bad one for a change, you'll quite understand, won't you?'

'It won't be a change,' said his aunt. 'Have you forgotten last term's report already? Shall I quote some of it for you?'

'No,' said Snubby hurriedly, suddenly remembering a few very nasty bits. He changed the subject. 'When do we go? I say, it'll be fun riding again, Aunt Susan – though I don't know if I'll be able to get on a horse now. My legs still feel peculiar.'

'Well, let the others ride then, and you wait till your legs let you mount,' said his aunt hard-heartedly. Snubby sighed. The time of being petted and fussed and coddled was over. He could see that. Well, it had been very nice while it lasted!

They all set off one day after breakfast. The three children looked pale, but they were in high spirits. It was fun to be going away to a strange place. Diana thought pityingly of her friends, swotting away at school. It was almost worth while having that awful 'flu, to be going away unexpectedly like this.

Mrs Lynton drove the car with Diana beside her. At the back were Roger, Snubby and, of course, Loony. Loony's great idea in a car was to stick his head as far out of the window as possible.

'Go faster, Aunt Susan,' urged Snubby. 'I want to see

what Loony does when his ears stand out straight behind him in the wind.'

'Don't talk to the driver,' said Diana. 'And don't let Loony hang out of the window too much. He'll get a chill.'

'He won't,' said Snubby. 'He never gets chills. He didn't even take the 'flu from us!'

They picked up Miss Pepper on the way, and then Diana went to sit at the back of the car with the two boys. They were all pleased to see the tall, trim woman, with her eyes twinkling as usual behind her glasses. She had a very nice smile that quite altered her rather prim face with the straight grey hair brushed away from it.

'The three children are not *quite* as lively as usual,' said Mrs Lynton, 'but you won't mind *that* of course. Loony, I fear, is much the same as ever – perhaps a little madder, if anything.'

Loony was delighted to see Miss Pepper. He put his paws up on the back of her seat and snuffled lovingly down her neck. Then he pawed at her hat and she clutched it in haste.

'Is Loony still fond of taking brushes away and hiding them?' she asked.

'Yes!' chorused the children. '*And* towels now too, Miss Pepper.'

Miss Pepper groaned and made a mental note to keep her towel in a drawer, and not hanging by her washbasin. She liked Loony but he really was a trial. She wondered how her cousin would put up with him. Oh dear – she hadn't thought of that!

It was a long drive to Ring O' Bells Village. They had a picnic on the way, and then, in the afternoon, Diana, Roger and Snubby lolled together in the back of the car and fell asleep. They were already tired with their journey. Loony stuck his head further and further out of the window, then his shoulders, and enjoyed himself thoroughly.

'We're getting near the village now,' said Miss Pepper, looking at the map on her lap. 'See those hills? Well, Ring O' Bells is behind them, on the south side, so it's very warm, though fairly high.'

They rounded the foot of the hills, and came in sight of the sprawling old village. The houses were made of white stone, and looked very solidly built indeed. The children woke up as they came into the village, a little way up the slope of the great hill.

'We're almost there,' said Miss Pepper, turning to them. 'Look – that's Hubbard Cottage. When I was here as a little girl I really thought Mother Hubbard lived there. And over there is a very old show-place called Ring O' Bells Hall – it was once a mansion, built in the six-teenth century. It's now on show to the public, with a lot of the old original furniture in it. It's got a secret passage too.'

'*Has* it!' said Diana in delight. 'Are the public allowed to see that, too, Miss Pepper?'

'Yes, on payment of an extra sixpence,' said Miss Pepper. 'They make a lot of money here in the summer-time, because people come from all over the place to see Ring O' Bells Village and hear its old legends. There are one or two old cottages in Ring O' Bells Wood that really might have been where Red Riding Hood lived!'

'Ring O' Bells Village – Ring O' Bells Wood,' said Diana. 'Mother Hubbard – Red Riding Hood – a secret passage! I say – this sounds exciting!'

'I dare say it's all quite ordinary to the people who live here,' said her mother. 'Look – there are the riding sta-bles. I'm sure you'll be there more than anywhere else, helping with the horses and getting yourselves even dirtier than usual!'

The riding stables looked nice. They too seemed old, and a bit tumbledown at the back, but the horses in the paddock were spruce and well groomed. The children felt their spirits rising high.

At last the car drew up in a lane off the main road, outside an old solid-looking stone house. It was quite big, and rather rambling, as it spread away at the back into an odd wing or two and some outbuildings. Hens ran over the garden, and ducks quacked from somewhere not far off. A dog ran barking to welcome them, its tail wagging furiously.

'A golden spaniel,' said Snubby, delighted. 'Hey, Loony – meet your cousin. Do you know his name, Miss Pepper?'

'Yes – it's Loopy,' said Miss Pepper, with a chuckle, and everyone roared with laughter. Loony and Loopy – what a pair of names – and what a pair of dogs too!

Loopy seemed practically as mad as Loony in the way he pranced about and barked and fawned over everyone. They might all have been long lost friends of his! Miss Pepper's cousin hurried out to greet them, smiling. She was like Miss Pepper, but shorter and fatter, and her smile was not quite so wide and cheerful. Still, the children thought she looked quite jolly – and anyway she had a very nice dog, who would be good company for Loony.

Soon they were all indoors, sitting down to a fine meal of home-made bread, scones and cakes, with home-made jam, and home-made honey in dishes. Mrs Lynton saw with approval that the three children seemed to have suddenly recovered their enormous appetites. Diana's cheeks began to glow a little and she chattered as fast as the boys.

Loony and Loopy sat impatiently beside first one child and then another, hoping for titbits. Occasionally they sniffed each other approvingly, though Loopy growled if Loony got a titbit he thought *he* ought to have.

'And now–' said Mrs Lynton when they had all finished, 'now, you three – you're to go straight to bed. You have had a long and tiring drive, and I can see that Snubby's legs are turning to jelly again.'

All three protested – but not very violently. Secretly they all longed to get between the sheets and lie down in comfort. Snubby felt surprised at himself for wanting such a peculiar thing, and wondered seriously whether he wasn't suddenly turning into an old man.

It wasn't long before they were all in bed, and Diana's eyes closed almost at once. She shared a bedroom with her mother that night, but Mrs Lynton was going off early the next morning, to drive herself home. Then Diana would have her room to herself. The boys shared one. Loony shared it too, of course. He would never be parted from Snubby at night.

'Have you got an old rug or something to put on Snubby's bed?' Miss Pepper asked her cousin. 'Just so that the dog won't spoil your nice blankets, you know. I'm afraid he *will* sleep on the boy's bed. I do hope you won't mind.'

'I would have minded last year,' said her cousin, producing an old rug from a chest. 'But since I've had to put up with Loopy I've learnt a lot of things. I won't let him sleep on my bed – but he insists on sleeping on my couch. Here you are, Becky – take it to Snubby. What a name!'

'It's because of his snub-nose,' said Miss Pepper, escaping with the rug. Snubby was already asleep. So was Diana. Roger opened his eyes just a little to say good night and then he too was asleep. His mother peeped in as Miss Pepper arranged the old rug on Snubby's bed for Loony to lie on.

'I do hope you'll all have a peaceful, restful time,' she

16

said. 'I shouldn't think anything much ever happens here, does it?'

'No, nothing,' said Miss Pepper. 'It's a funny old dreamy, half-forgotten place. We shan't have any excitement at all!'

She shouldn't have said that. It was just *ask*ing for things to happen, of course!

Chapter Three

Mother Hubbard's Cottage

For once, not one of the children awoke early. Mrs Lynton was away before even Snubby had opened his eyes! They didn't even hear her car purring down the lane, and they didn't hear the hens clucking, Loopy barking, or the rooks cawing as they sailed overhead.

Snubby only woke because Loony insisted. Loony was tired of hearing everyone awake and astir, and of being shut up in a bedroom with two sleeping boys. He scraped at the door but nobody came. He heard Loopy barking and suddenly gave a loud answering bark.

Snubby awoke with a jump, but Roger went on sleeping peacefully, his head under the bedclothes. Snubby sat up and looked at the time. Twenty-five-past *nine!* Good gracious! Whoever heard of such a thing? He leapt out of bed, quite forgetting to test his legs as he usually did, since they had become so curiously jelly-like. However, they behaved very well, and didn't let him down or even wobble. He went to the window, Loony licking him madly, his tail wagging nineteen to the dozen.

It was a brilliant morning in early May. Snubby's bedroom looked out on the back garden of the house, and there was plenty to see there! Dozens of hens scrabbled about. Three great geese cackled in a corner. Ducks swam on a round pond in the field just outside the garden, upending themselves in their usual ridiculous way.

A cat sat sunning itself on a wall, keeping a wary eye open for Loopy, who was always under the impression that he could leap any wall. He couldn't, but the cat was always afraid that he might. It stuck one leg up in the air and began to give itself a thorough morning wash.

'Now this is just the kind of place I *like*,' said Snubby, rubbing his hands. 'Plenty going on. Is that a goat I see beyond the duck pond – and two little kids? And surely that's a grey donkey? I'll have a ride on him today.'

'Woof,' said Loony, trying his hardest to see out of the window too. Snubby lifted him up. He caught sight of Loopy down below, sniffing hard at a smell of some sort, and almost leapt out of the window in his excitement. His sudden barking awoke Roger.

'Come on, Roger, get up!' said Snubby eagerly. 'It's awfully late. This is a wizard place. All kinds of animals and things. Loopy's down there, longing for Loony to join him.'

'Well, let him then,' said Roger, fending off Loony as he tried to cover him with licks. 'Can't you teach your dog to stop washing everyone he loves? I'm dripping already. Shut up, Loony, keep your tongue in your mouth!'

Snubby opened the bedroom door, and Loony shot downstairs, taking the stairs in almost one bound. He slid across the polished hall on his four feet, neatly avoided a little table there, and gave Miss Pepper a real shock as she came in from the garden. Before she could say a word, Loony was hob-nobbing excitedly with Loopy, who at once began to show off.

'Couple of mad creatures,' said Miss Pepper to herself. 'I suppose that means that the children are now awake.'

Judging by the thuds upstairs, they were. Miss Pepper called to her cousin, 'Hannah! The children are awake at last. I'll get the milk out of the fridge for them. They do so love it icy-cold.'

'Oooh,' said Snubby, who in two minutes' time appeared dressed at the dining-room door, and was gazing

19

with joy at the table. 'Ham and tomatoes! And what's this? Hot sausage rolls! For *breakfast!* I say – are we going to be fed up, like the doctor said? I heard him tell Aunt Susan to feed us up well.'

'Yes – you're going to be fed up,' said Miss Pepper, smiling. 'I hope I shan't be – by the end of these few days here!'

'Ha ha – joke!' said Snubby politely. He sat down. 'I don't need to wait for the others, do I? Do I begin with porridge?'

'You do,' said Miss Pepper, serving him out of a dish on the food-warmer. 'And take plenty of cream – plenty! Doctor's orders. You've gone skinny and I don't like you skinny.'

'Gosh! Can I really take as much cream as I like?' said Snubby, reaching for the big jug with its pattern of flowers all down it. 'All my life people have been telling me to go carefully with the cream!'

Hannah Pepper came in after a while to see that everything was all right. She seemed pleased to see the three children tucking in. 'They won't be long putting a bit of flesh on again,' she said to her cousin, who was now knitting by the window. 'But don't let the dog have any cream. He's fat enough as it is.'

'He's only licking a drip off my fingers,' said Snubby. 'Hallo, here's Loopy. Have a lick, Loopy?'

But cream was no luxury to Loopy, and he disdained it. He sniffed at Loony's mouth to smell what other food he had received. Loopy was very ready to welcome Loony, but he didn't mean him to have anything more than his fair share!

'Can we go and have a snoop round the place, Miss Pepper?' asked Diana, when they could not possibly eat any more. 'You don't need to come,' she added hastily, feeling that it would be nicer to snoop round by themselves. 'And is there a book about Ring O' Bells we could read? A guide book or something?'

'No. But I dare say the woman at the old mansion we passed yesterday – Ring O' Bells Hall, it's called – can tell you all you want to know,' said Miss Pepper. 'Can't she, Hannah?'

'Yes, she can,' said her cousin, who was now clearing away the breakfast things. 'It's a pity she's not a native here – she's a stranger really, who read up all about the old place, and put in for the job as caretaker and guide to Ring O' Bells Hall when it was decided to open it as a show-place. Still, she certainly knows all the history of the place, and explains it very well – better, maybe, than one of the villagers could have done it.'

'We'll go and have a good look all round,' said Roger, feeling the sun warm on his face, as it streamed through the window. 'I'm going to enjoy this unexpected holiday. Can Loopy come with us, Miss Hannah?'

'Oh, *yes*,' said Miss Hannah thankfully. 'Do take him. He's under my feet all the time, and he *will* keep running off with the mats. Now just look out of the window – if he hasn't got somebody's towel too this morning!'

Snubby had a feeling that it was Loony not Loopy who was responsible for the sudden appearance of the towel. He got up in a hurry to fetch it, only to meet Loony running through the hall with another towel dragging behind him!

'Loony! This is not your home!' scolded Snubby, in a low voice. 'It's somebody else's place. If you start dragging towels about, you'll be sent away. Do you hear? Then we shall play with Loopy, not with *you!*'

Loony's tail went down, and he put on his most mournful expression. Snubby put the two towels back in their places, and went downstairs. This time he met Loopy carrying a mat in his mouth, evidently taken from the dining room, where there were many rugs laid down to cover the old wooden floor.

Snubby didn't interfere with Loopy. Let him take his own rugs! It was no business of Snubby's. Anyway, the more mischief Loopy got up to, the less Loony's mischief would be noticed!

The three children set off together. They went down the sunny lane, already sweet with the scent of the first drifts of may blossom. Cowslips danced in the nearby fields, and primroses lined the ditches by the road. The brilliant blue of the germander speedwell shone beneath the hedges. What a lovely place Ring O' Bells was!

They came to the white stone cottage that Miss Pepper had called Hubbard Cottage. The name was on the gate. The children stood there staring. They supposed Mother Hubbard might have lived *some*where when she was alive – and why not here?

The door opened and an old woman in a red shawl and printed skirt appeared, shaking a duster. She looked so exactly like Mother Hubbard that the children gazed in delight. She smiled at them.

'You visitors here?' she said in a pleasant brogue. 'You've brought the good weather with you!'

Loopy scrabbled at the gate, trying to get in. This sounded like the kind of old woman who was generous with titbits. Loony put his paws on the middle bar and looked through.

'Ah – there's Loopy,' said the old woman. 'I'll find him a bone – and one for the other dog too.'

'She really *might* be Mother Hubbard,' said Diana in excitement. 'I wonder if *she's* got a dog. We'll ask her.'

They opened the gate and went up the tiny stone path, edged with polyanthus and wallflowers, and stood at the little door, waiting. They peered inside the cottage. It was dim, and they could hardly make out anything.

'Come away in,' cried a voice, and they went cautiously in, their eyes finding it difficult to get accustomed to the dim light after the brilliant May sunshine outside.

The front door opened straight into a little room. Mother Hubbard, as they all called her, was in a room beyond. Diana clutched Roger's arm. 'Look – the cupboard!' she whispered. 'She's got a cupboard!'

Mother Hubbard was at an open cupboard, that went back into the thick stone wall of the cottage. But it wasn't bare! It was filled with pans and dishes and jugs of all kinds – it was, in fact, her larder, set in the cool stone wall. She brought out two bones for the dogs.

'Did you ever have a dog?' asked Diana suddenly as the old lady came back into the sitting room, or parlour.

'Dear me, no,' said Mother Hubbard, looking surprised at the sudden question. 'Not of my own, if that's what you mean. I've lived with my old grandad nearly all my life, and he don't like dogs, never did. I like them, mind you – I've always got a bone for one that comes along. Old Grandad don't mind, so long as they don't go worriting him out in the garden there.'

It was astonishing to hear this 'Old Mother Hubbard' actually had a grandfather out in the garden. 'Could we see him?' asked Roger. 'I expect he's very interesting, isn't he? He could go a long way back in history, couldn't he?'

'Well, he says he's over a hundred years old,' said Mother Hubbard. 'He's asleep now, look – you come and talk to him some other time. He knows a rare lot about Ring O' Bells – more than that woman at Ring O' Bells has ever read or heard of, I can tell you *that!*'

This was interesting, and rather exciting. 'We'll certainly come back!' said Roger. 'And thanks most awfully for the bones!'

Chapter Four

Ring O' Bells Hall

As the children went past the strange little 'Mother Hubbard' Cottage, they peeped over the high garden wall of stone, just to see if they could spy 'Old Grandad' there.

They saw a tiny old man fast asleep in a chair, propped up with cushions. A long clay pipe dangled in one gnarled, wrinkled hand. He had a little fringe of fluffy white hair round his head, which otherwise was quite pink and bald. His nose was a mere button, but his eyebrows made up for that. They jutted out fiercely and shaggily, snow-white and thick, almost hiding his closed eyes.

'He looks fierce, except for his nose,' said Diana in a low voice. 'Look at his mouth, with its stuck-out lower lip, and his chin with the funny bit of white beard on it. Do you suppose he really *is* a hundred years old?'

'He looks *two* hundred,' said Snubby. 'Get down, Loony, you ass. I warn you, Grandad won't stand any nonsense from a silly young thing like *you*. Get hold of Loopy, Di – he looks as if he's going to leap over the wall.'

'We'll certainly come back and talk to him,' said Roger. 'A hundred years old! The things he could remember! He's a bit of living history.'

They went on their way, and soon came to Ring O' Bells Hall. It was a big, grand building, but rather grim looking, built of such solid grey-white stone that it looked as if not even a bomb would disturb it.

It had two towers, one square, and one round, which seemed peculiar to the children. A stone-flagged path led up to the great door, which was studded with iron nails. It was open.

The children went in with the dogs. A cold voice greeted them. 'Dogs not allowed inside, please. Tie them up outside.'

'But they'll bark their heads off!' protested Snubby.

'Then don't come in yourselves,' said the voice. At first they could not see who was speaking, because the great hall of the building was dark, lit only by a slit of a window at one end, and the dim light that came through the front door.

Then they saw that there was a table set at one side of the hall, and a woman sat there, knitting. She was dressed very neatly in plain black, and her grey hair was strained away from her white face, and put into a bun at the back. She was rather shapeless, and her hands looked very big and bony as she clicked her knitting needles in and out.

The children didn't like her face very much. The mouth was set in what was meant to be a smile, but the small black eyes above it were hard and unsmiling as they looked over at the three children and the dogs. How old was she? She might have been any age, Diana thought.

'We thought we might see round the Hall,' she said, at last. 'Are we allowed to?'

'Yes, but not with the dogs,' said the woman. 'Not allowed, as I told you. This place has some very valuable old furniture and ornaments in it, and no animals are allowed inside. They might cause great damage.'

'Well, that's fair enough, I suppose,' said Roger, and he took Loony and Loopy outside. They didn't mind going in the least, because neither of them liked the great cold Hall, nor the small cold woman. Roger tied them to a post, put their bones down beside them, and left them, hoping that they wouldn't begin barking.

They paid their fees to the woman. She put down her

25

knitting, rolled up her wool, and wrote down the sums of money in her big account book, which lay open before her.

Then she got up. The children followed her round the mansion. It felt a dead, forgotten place, and everywhere struck cold, that lovely warm May morning. Diana shivered. She didn't like any of it much.

The woman recited long strings of facts about the old place, but she didn't make them sound very interesting.

'In 1645 Hugh Dourley lived in this Hall, and it was he who first caused it to be called Ring O' Bells,' she droned on.

'Why?' asked Snubby, his interest caught at last.

'He had a peal of bells put in the south tower,' said the woman, beginning to gabble. 'He rang them when he had anything to rejoice about. But one night they rang themselves, so it's said – and it wasn't because there was anything to rejoice about, either. His eldest son had been killed, and he didn't know. But the bells rang at the very moment of his death.'

This sounded rather weird. The children were now at the bottom of the square south tower. A small spiral stairway went up, and they wondered if they might climb it.

'Yes, climb up if you want to,' said the woman. 'You'll see the bells hanging there, high up. They say they're still the same ones that Hugh Dourley put in, but it stands to reason they can't be.'

The children climbed up the stairway. It was steep and narrow and twisted sharply, so that it was difficult to climb without slipping.

At the top of the stairway was a small platform. The children looked up, and saw, high above their heads, a cluster of bells, hanging silently on what looked like thick ropes.

Snubby stared at the bells, and his hands itched to ring them. Snubby always liked anything that made a loud noise.

'Can we ring them?' he asked, feeling, of course, perfectly certain of the answer.

The guide-woman looked shocked. 'Of course not,' she said. 'Whatever would people think?'

'I don't know,' said Snubby. 'We could ring the bells and find out.'

'There aren't any ropes to *ring* the bells,' said Diana. Sure enough, there were no long ropes hanging down to the little platform they stood on. The bells hung high up on their own short ropes, and there was no way of ringing them at all.

'They'll never ring again,' said the guide. 'People say they'll ring only when enemies come to Ring O' Bells, but that's nonsense. How can bells ring if there's nothing to peal them with?'

'And what enemies could come here, to this little out-of-the-way place?' said Diana. 'Roger, isn't this a strange tower, with its tiny spiral staircase, and its long-forgotten bells, unable to ring ever again.'

'You sound very dismal,' said Roger. 'Like me to throw a stone and make one of the bells ring?'

'Now, now,' said the woman sharply. 'Don't talk like that or I shall have to ask you to go.'

'I'm only joking,' said Roger, grinning. 'What else is there to see?'

The history of the old place was full of boring recitals of this person and that person, who happened to have lived in the house. The children followed the guide about, yawning, but one piece of information made them prick up their ears.

'The Lady Paulet had a secret chamber made in the fireplace here,' droned the guide, as she took them into

27

a small room with an enormous fireplace. All the rooms had big, old-fashioned fireplaces. The children had actually been able to stand upright in some of them, their heads and shoulders up the wide chimney. There was no soot, because it was years now since Ring O' Bells had been lived in.

'A secret chamber!' said Roger. 'Where?' He gazed at the big fireplace, and could not imagine where any secret room could be.

'Look up the chimney,' said the guide. 'You will see what looks like two steps there, cut in the wall of the chimney. If you go up those steps, and then put out your hand, you will feel a cavity behind the fireplace there. It is big enough for a man to step inside and hide.'

'Can we go and see?' asked Snubby, eagerly, visualising a proper little secret room, with perhaps a small table and a bench, as dark as pitch.

'If you like,' said the woman, and she produced a torch, which she held out to them. Roger went first. He shone the torch up the wide chimney, and saw the two rough steps hewn there in the side. He climbed up and began to feel about for the cavity the woman had mentioned. He soon found it. It was a fairly big hole, taller than he was, and he found that he could easily step into it.

But that was all he could do! There was no room for anything except just his own body! It wasn't so much a secret room, as a secret place to hide in, just big enough to take a man – and woe betide him if there should happen to be a fire on the hearth!

'He'd be suffocated, or would be cooked,' thought Roger, getting down thankfully, and handing the torch to Diana. He gave her a shove up. She didn't like the cavity at all when she felt it and shone her torch there. She wouldn't go into it.

'Ugh! It's horrid!' she said. 'It feels so dirty too. Fancy

hiding there! Why, it would only just about take a grown-up.'

Snubby went next, and he, of course, insisted on squeezing himself right into the cavity, and feeling all round it, just in *case* there was something else to find. But there wasn't. It was just what it was meant to be – a temporary hiding-place for some man in danger. Snubby found that he could sit down in it too. The others got impatient and called to him. 'Snubby! Come along! You'll get filthy.'

Roger was very dirty through getting into the cavity. He hadn't realised it might be so filthy. As for Snubby, when he finally jumped down on to the big stone hearth, and appeared before the others, they could hardly believe their eyes. He looked like a sweep!

'I say – Miss Pepper's going to have something to say to you,' said Diana. 'Keep away from me, for goodness' sake. You look awful – and you smell awful too. Just like you to get dirtier than anyone else, Snubby. Keep *away* from me, I said!'

Snubby blew down at himself, feeling rather dismayed to see his coating of dirt. He glanced at the guide and caught a look of pleasure on her face. 'Horrid old thing!' he thought. 'She only encouraged us to get into that cavity because she thought we'd get black, and be told off when we got home.'

He went near to her and banged himself violently as if to get rid of the dust and soot. Some flew over her, and she started back in disgust.

'You'd better go home and clean up,' she said.

'Oh, no!' said Snubby at once. 'OH, no! We haven't seen the thing we want to see most – the secret passage. Where is that? We want to see it, please.'

Chapter Five

The Secret Passage

'No – you go off home and clean yourselves,' said the woman crossly. 'I've had enough of you. You'll mess up all the clean rooms if you go about like that now.'

'Well, it was your fault,' said Snubby, banging himself violently again, and making the soot fly. 'You must have known that place was filthy. Come on – we paid you an extra sixpence each to show us the passage. Where is it?'

'You come back clean tomorrow and I'll show it to you,' said the woman. But Snubby could be very obstinate when he wanted to.

'I'll walk all over the Ring O' Bells Hall banging off my soot, if you don't show us,' he announced, and gave himself such a blow on the chest that everyone sneezed because of the soot.

The woman scowled and said no more. She went back to the hall and took a bunch of keys from a hook. She selected one and led the way to a panelled room, which she unlocked.

'The secret passage was made in the year 1748,' she said. 'Or so the chronicles say. This room was panelled then, and an entrance to the passage was made behind the panelling. It runs behind it for a little way, and then curves downwards into the foundations of the house.'

'Does it go to the cellars?' asked Roger.

'No. It avoids those, and ends blindly,' said the guide.

'What was the use of it then, if it didn't lead anywhere?' asked Snubby. 'What a pity!'

'It was probably used as a hiding-place,' said the guide.

'More people could crowd into it than into the small cavity behind the fireplace. Now – can any of you find the secret passage?'

They looked round the panelled room. It was dark, because the windows were heavily leaded and not very large. The ivy that grew outside obscured the light even more.

Snubby began tapping over the panelling. He gave a triumphant cry at last. 'It sounds awfully hollow here! Tap it, you others. Then tap this bit. Can you hear the difference?'

They could. One panel sounded hollow, the other sounded solid. The woman watched them, looking bored.

But Snubby could not find out how to enter the secret passage. He pushed this and pulled that, but nothing happened at all. He turned to the woman at last.

'Tell us where it is exactly. It's very cleverly hidden.'

'Watch,' said the woman, and she went to an enormous tapestry picture over the mantelpiece. The children went with her. 'But the panelling sounds solid all round here,' protested Snubby. 'We tapped it.'

The woman said nothing. She reached up to the dim face in the old picture. The face wore a helmet, or what looked like a helmet, pushed back over its forehead. The woman pressed a stud in the helmet and then stood back.

The great picture slid silently to one side – about four inches only – but enough to show a small panel of wood that looked just a little different from the others.

The woman put her hand firmly on the small panel and pressed it to one side. It slid along under her hand, leaving a tiny space, just big enough for a hand to go into it.

'Feel inside the space,' she said. They all groped there, feeling curiously excited as they did so. There was something mysterious about this – a secret planned long ago

31

by a clever brain, a secret well hidden, and perhaps of great use more than two centuries before.

Each of them felt a knob in the space behind. 'Now you – press it,' said the guide, tapping Roger on the arm. He pressed the knob hard and it yielded suddenly beneath his hand. At the same moment something rattled softly behind the panelling not far off.

'That knob releases a lever which in turn enables us to press back a bigger panel,' said the woman, going to the panelling from behind which the rattle had come. She pressed her hand against a big panel, and it gradually slid into the wall, sliding neatly behind the panel next to it. A hole yawned there at last, big enough for a man to squeeze into. The woman shone her torch into the hole.

'There you are,' she said. 'Not much to see, really. Just a passage behind the panelling. It runs along beside it for a few feet and then goes downwards to the blind end I spoke of.'

'I want to go inside,' said Snubby, of course, and he put one leg into the hole.

The woman pulled him back roughly. 'No!' she said. 'No one is allowed to go inside. Now surely you don't want to get dirtier than you are! Get back at once.'

Snubby struggled away, and tried his hardest to get into the dark hole. He badly wanted to follow that secret passage. Why did it go to a blind end? Was it only a hiding-place, then, not a passage? He didn't believe it.

The woman got angry. 'I shall report you,' she said, still holding Snubby by his coat. 'Do you want me to lose my job? Now, you just do as you're told. And listen to those dogs of yours barking! Something's up. You'd better go and see what's the matter.'

Snubby heard Loony and Loopy barking and he reluctantly got back into the room. But he made up his mind about one thing – he was going to explore that secret passage before his holiday was ended!

All three rushed out into the front garden of Ring O' Bells Hall to see what was exciting the dogs. It was only another dog! He had come trotting by, and had smelt the two bones belonging to Loony and Loopy. He had also seen that the other two dogs were tied up.

He had apparently nipped up to them and taken one of the bones before either Loony or Loopy had seen him. Then he had sat himself down well out of reach and proceeded to crunch up the bone.

This, of course, made the two spaniels go nearly off their heads with rage and desperation, and if their leads had not been very strong, there is no doubt that the four-footed thief would have been chased out of the country!

As it was, all they could do was to bark madly, almost strangling themselves with their leads. Snubby ran at the thief-dog, and he tore off, leaving the bone behind him.

'Take your dogs away,' called the woman from the door of Ring O' Bells Hall. 'And don't come here again with them. Anyway, you've seen all there is to see.'

The children went off, the dogs still on the lead, straining after the scent left behind by the other dog. Snubby got cross. 'Stop it, Loony – you're almost pulling my arm out. You've got your bone back, so what's all the excitement about?'

Diana suddenly looked white. Roger noticed it and took her arm. 'Come on, old girl,' he said, 'we'll get back. This is the first day since the 'flu that we've taken much exercise or had much excitement. You looked fagged out. Lean on me and we'll go home.'

They were all very glad to get back to the house. Miss Pepper was there, looking out for them. Lunch was being laid, but alas, none of them felt quite like it after their rather peculiar morning.

'You all look very tired,' said Miss Pepper reproachfully. 'Whatever have you been up to?'

'Only talking to old Mother Hubbard and getting the dogs a bone, and seeing over Ring O' Bells Hall,' said Snubby, sinking down into a chair. 'And examining secret hidey-holes in fireplaces and secret passages behind panels and–'

'Oh, Snubby! You surely haven't been doing all that?' said Miss Pepper. 'And what in the world has made you so dirty? *Look* how dirty you've made that cushion. You look as if you've been up a chimney or something.'

'Good guess!' said Snubby. 'Oh, Miss Pepper – *must* I go and change and have a bath and all that? I do suddenly feel so tired.'

He wasn't pretending. Miss Pepper patted him kindly, and then was horrified to find a cloud of sooty dust rising into the air out of his shoulder. Dear, dear – trust Snubby to arrive home in some sort of dirty state. But she hadn't the heart to make him change even his coat.

They ate rather a poor lunch, mostly because they had had a late and very good breakfast. Then they dragged themselves off to have a rest in their beds. Snubby managed to undress himself and throw his sooty things down to Miss Pepper. Then, rolled round in his dressing gown, he fell fast asleep.

'That 'flu really did take it out of them, poor things,' said Miss Pepper to her cousin Hannah, as they sat sewing together peacefully that afternoon. There wasn't a sound to be heard from the children. Loony was on Snubby's bed, of course, and Loopy was out in the garden, making futile leaps at the cat on the wall.

'You've done enough walking for today,' said Miss Pepper firmly, when the children came down to tea, showing signs of a healthy appetite. 'Just potter about the

34

garden after tea. You can feed the chickens for Miss Hannah and collect the eggs.'

However, Loony and Loopy made up for the lack of energy on the part of the children, by indulging to the full their craze for purloining mats, towels and brushes, and when the children arrived back in the garden after feeding the hens, and looking for eggs, they found half the mats and towels in the house strewn over the grass. Somebody's hairbrush sat in the middle of a clump of polyanthus!

Loony got a spanking with the hairbrush and retired under the sofa, sulking. Loopy, who had never seen anyone spanked with a hairbrush before, rushed away in horror and didn't appear till suppertime.

'By the way,' said Miss Pepper, at supper, 'do you ever hear from that strange friend of yours – Barney. He was a circus boy, wasn't he – and had a monkey called Miranda.'

'Yes,' said Roger. 'We don't *very* often hear from him. He's been all over the place since we last saw him. We ought to hear soon, though. Good old Barney.'

'Who's this?' asked Miss Hannah, with interest. 'Barney? I've not heard of him before.'

'Oh, he's a circus boy we made friends with,' said Roger. 'He's a nice chap. Mother likes him, so you can guess he's all right. He's got no mother, but he's hoping to find his father one day. He's got one somewhere – an actor, he thinks. But you should see Miranda, his monkey.'

'No thank you,' said Miss Hannah, with a shudder. 'I can't bear the nasty little things. I hope you won't hear from your friend just yet, anyway, if he's got a monkey.'

But they did hear from Barney – the very next day too.

Chapter Six

News from Barney

The three children didn't wake quite so late the next day. In fact, though rather on the late side, they were down for breakfast with Miss Pepper and Miss Hannah.

And by Roger's plate was a letter in Barney's characteristic handwriting – large, sprawling, slanting all over the envelope! Good, good, good!

Roger snatched it up. 'I say – a letter from old Barney! Funny we should have been talking about him last night. I wonder if there's any chance of seeing him.'

He tore open the envelope and read the letter aloud, with Diana and Snubby hanging on every word.

'DEAR ROGER,

Just to say I'm out of a job again after a very good one indeed. What do you think I've been doing? Looking after a troupe of monkeys in a circus! Right up my street, of course. Miranda's had a grand time – putting on no end of airs, and bossing all the monkeys in the troupe.

Well, I made a good bit of money, and I thought it would be nice to see you all again. The only thing is – won't you have gone back to school by now? If you have, it's no use, of course, and I'll have to try and see you all in the summer. But if you're not back yet, let me know, and I'll hitch-hike along to you, no matter how many miles it is. Can't neglect my old friends like this too long, else they'll be forgetting me!

So long – and here's hoping to see you.

BARNEY.

Miranda sends warm love.'

36

All three looked at one another in glee. 'Good old Barney! Dear old Barney! We'll have to get him along here to Ring O'Bells Village, and see him again for a bit. What a bit of luck we aren't back at school yet!' Roger rubbed his hands joyfully.

'Barney can't come here with his monkey,' said Miss Hannah firmly. 'I'm having no monkeys in my house. If the boy likes to ask someone to look after his monkey for him, I'd be pleased to have him here, for your sake – but no monkey. That's flat.'

'Oh!' said all three. They knew perfectly well that nothing in the world would persuade Barney to leave Miranda with anyone else. It was quite unthinkable.

'He could perhaps lodge somewhere in the village,' said Miss Pepper, seeing the children's disappointed faces.

'Yes. Though as it's May and so fine and warm he'd probably just as soon sleep out of doors,' said Diana, remembering that Barney didn't need a roof over his head, as ordinary people did. 'He'll find a barn or haystack or something.'

'Very well,' said Miss Hannah. 'But I will not have the monkey here. Becky, you'll see that it doesn't come here, won't you?'

Miss Pepper nodded at her cousin. 'Yes, Hannah. Don't worry – the monkey shan't come here – though it's not a bad little thing at all. I didn't mind it after a bit.'

Miss Hannah gave a mild snort. 'Well, I should never, never take to a monkey,' she said. 'And at my time of life I'm not going to try.'

The children went out into the garden after they had made their beds and tidied up. Diana took her fountain pen, and Roger had note-paper and envelopes. Snubby, as usual, merely looked on and made unhelpful remarks about what to say to Barney.

'Dear Barney,' wrote Diana:

'Thanks awfully for your letter. You'll be surprised at our address, but we've had 'flu, and we've all been sent away here for a change, Snubby and Loony too. Loony didn't have the 'flu though, of course. There's a dog here, called Loopy, who's very good company for Loony, because he's just as idiotic.'

'Tell Barney how he takes all the mats out,' put in Snubby.

Diana took no notice. 'I wonder if I've spelt "idiotic" right,' she said. 'Yes, I think I have. I'll go on now.'

She went on with the letter, with Roger and Snubby looking over her shoulder, breathing down her neck.

'We all felt pretty awful after the 'flu, and . . .' she went on writing. Snubby interrupted.

'Tell him my legs felt just like jelly,' he said.

'*Do* you think that would interest him?' said Diana scornfully. 'Who cares about your jelly-legs? And do stop panting down my neck. You feel like Loony.'

Loony heard his name and bounced up at her, so that her pen made a deep mark across the letter. 'Blow you, Loony – it was such a nice neat letter and now look what you've done. Anyway, Barney will guess it was you. Get down!'

'Go on, Di – you've just written: "We all felt pretty awful after the 'flu," ' said Roger. 'Are you going to tell him how to get here? He won't have any notion of where this place is.'

'If he's going to hitch-hike, what's the good of telling him?' asked Diana. 'I'll just say, "Show this address to anyone you're hitch-hiking with, and they'll tell you if you're going in the right direction or not." '

'Tell him about the secret passage,' said Snubby. 'He'll like that.'

'You seem to think I'm writing a *book* or something.' said Diana, exasperated. 'And *will* you stop breathing down my neck. I'm going to end the letter now. It's long enough already.'

She finished it. 'We're here with Miss Pepper, you remember her, don't you? We're staying with her cousin, Miss Hannah, who doesn't like monkeys, so you won't be able to stay with us, worse luck. But we can arrange something when we see you. Lots of love to darling Miranda

Your friends,

Diana, Roger and Snubby.

P.S. – Loony sends his best woof.'

They all signed their names, and Diana heaved a sigh of relief. 'There – that's done. I do hate writing letters, but it's nice to be able to tell Barney to come. *What* a bit of luck we're not back at school!'

They posted the letter, and speculated for some time as to when Barney would get to them. 'He'll get our letter tomorrow,' said Roger. 'And maybe he'll start straight away. If he hitch-hikes as cleverly as he usually does, he might be here any time after tomorrow.'

This was very cheering. Everyone felt much better somehow, now that they could look forward to seeing Barney and Miranda.

They pictured Barney's wide-set startlingly blue eyes in his brown face, and Miranda's dear little monkey face. Yes – it really would be fine to see them both again.

On the way back from the post, they passed Mother Hubbard's Cottage. The old lady was out in the garden, picking polyanthus. She smiled at them.

'Good morning, Mother Hubbard,' said Snubby, quite forgetting it wasn't her real name. Roger and Diana gave him a punch, one each side. He was taken aback. 'Oh – er – I mean – well, good morning, Mam!'

The old lady laughed. 'Call me Mother Hubbard if you like,' she said. 'It's no matter to me what I'm called. And I've certainly got a cupboard, though it isn't bare.'

'Is your Grandad asleep today?' asked Roger, remembering the old, old man with his fierce, shaggy eyebrows and fluff of white hair round his head.

'I'll see,' said Mother Hubbard, and disappeared. She soon came back. 'No, he's not asleep,' she said. 'You go out and talk to him. He's got a wonderful memory, though he repeats himself sometimes. He remembers what happened years ago, better than what happens these days. Why, he forgets what he had for dinner as soon as he's eaten it, poor old man!'

They had to leave Loony and Loopy tied up outside, of course. Old Grandad didn't like dogs. Mother Hubbard took them out of her back door into the little garden beyond. Old Grandad was there, sitting up in his cushioned chair, smoking a long clay pipe.

'Good morning,' said the three children, marvelling again at his immense eyebrows. They could hardly see his eyes because of them. They wondered how *he* could see. Diana secretly thought that he looked a little like an old English sheepdog, with its shaggy hair over its eyes!

'Good morning to you all,' said Old Grandad, and pointed with his clay pipe to the ground. 'Sit you down, and tell me your names and who you be. I've not set eyes on you before.'

They told him their names. He chuckled when he heard Snubby's. 'Ah, they call you that acause of your turn-up nose, don't they? And do you see *my* nose? Button of a thing it is – and so they used to call me Button. And Button I be now, to my pals – Button Dourley, I am, and Button Dourley I'll die. I misremember my rightful name.

40

Mebbe it was John, mebbe it was Joe. But my nose named me, just like your nose named *you*!' And the old fellow pointed his pipe at Snubby and went off into a peculiar cackle of laughter, rather like a hen makes when she has laid an egg.

What he said interested the children very much. They sat up, all ears, when he told them his name. It wasn't the 'Button' so much, it was the surname – Dourley. Where had they heard it before? It rang a bell in the mind of each of them.

Diana remembered first. 'Hugh Dourley!' she said, out loud. 'Of course – Hugh Dourley.'

The old man heard her, and his shaggy eyebrows drew down even farther over his eyes. He pointed his pipe at Diana.

'That's my name you said just now, young lady! It was Hugh – that's right. It wasn't John or Joe – it was Hugh. How come I forgot it? But how do you know that, young lady?'

Diana was remembering how she had heard the woman at Ring O' Bells Hall telling the history of the old mansion. What was it she had said? Oh, yes! 'In 1645 Hugh Dourley lived in this Hall, and it was he who first caused it to be called Ring O'Bells,' she had droned.

Diana answered Old Grandad. 'We heard there was a Hugh Dourley who put in the bells at Ring O' Bells Hall,' she said. 'It's such an unusual name – Dourley – I remembered that long-ago Hugh Dourley, when you said *your* surname was Dourley. That's all.'

The old man had sunk back into his chair. His eyes were closed all but a slit.

He opened them suddenly and leaned over to children as if he had a secret to tell. 'Hugh Dourley was my Great-great-great-great-grandad,' he half-whispered. 'I don't know how many Greats. Yes, I'm one of the Dourleys of

Ring O'Bells. I know all about that old place – I know things nobody else knows. Maybe I'll tell you a few – just a few. Shall I?'

Chapter Seven

Old Grandad Talks

The three children were thrilled beyond words. They looked at Old Grandad, and at last Diana spoke.

'Would you really tell us about Ring O'Bells Hall? It's such an old, mysterious place – full of secrets. We saw that secret chamber in the old fireplace, and–'

'Oh that,' said Grandad scornfully. 'That's a poor thing. I doubt if anyone ever hid up there.'

'And we saw how the tapestry moved, so that the lever could be worked to free that big panel,' said Snubby. 'But the woman there wouldn't let us get into the secret passage behind.'

'Ah, many's the time I've been in that,' said Old Grandad, with a chuckle.

'What's the use of it?' asked Roger. 'Was it just a hiding-place, not really a passage? Does it go to a blind end, as the woman said?'

'A blind end!' said the old man, astonished. 'No, that it doesn't. Blind end indeed! What would be the good of that? No, no, young sir – that was a way of escape from the house centuries ago. Times were good and bad in those days, just like they are now – and the folks at Ring O' Bells never knew when enemies might come – or gangs of roaming thieves – or folks after revenge. Those were cruel days, so I've heard my old Grandad say.'

'*Your* old Grandad!' said Diana, in amazement. 'Good gracious – that must go right back into history. How old were you when your Grandad told you these tales?'

'That's getting on for a hundred years ago now,' said

the old man. 'Victoria was on the throne, and a bonny little woman she was too. It's said she visited Ring O' Bells once, but I misremember that.'

'Do go on,' said Diana. 'How old was your Grandad when he told you these tales?'

'Oh, he were a youngster,' said the old man with a curious high chuckle. 'He were only sixty mebbe, or thereabouts. But he'd heard plenty from *his* old Granny, and the tales he told you wouldn't believe!'

The children stared at him, watching his eyes go slit-like under their shaggy eyebrows as he wandered far away back into a past that seemed as near to him as the present day of May sunshine and warmth. How curious to be so old – how strange to read the pages of history in your own mind, instead of in a book!

Diana patted the gnarled old hand softly. 'Are we making you tired?' she said. 'Can you tell us any more? What did your Grandad's old Granny tell *him*?'

The old man began to pour out a jumble of strange tales. 'In the days when there were wolves round about here,' he began, and immediately they seemed to be back in Red Riding Hood's time!

'In the days when there were wolves, there came a hard winter. Ground were so hard that my old Grandad said sparks could be knocked out of it if so be you hammered it! But that's a tale, o' course. Well, one night the wolves came in a howling flock to Ring O'Bells, looking for cattle, looking for chickens, aye, and looking for humans too.'

'How horrible!' said Diana, with a shudder. 'Surely this must be long long ago?'

'I told you, it were in my Grandad's Granny's time,' said the old man, impatient at being interrupted. 'Folks were asleep, and the wolves got nearer. They got to

Mother Barlow's cottage in Ring O' Bells Wood, and they smelled the old woman. And there they stood, howling—'

Old Grandad leaned forward suddenly in his chair, making the children jump. 'And what do you suppose happened?' he said, his cracked old voice rising high. 'Why, them bells in Ring O'Bells Hall rang out loud and clear! They did so – loud they rang, and woke everyone up.'

He sank back, and said no more. 'And I suppose the people heard the wolves howling, when they awoke, and went to drive them off, and rescued poor Mother Barlow?' asked Diana, after a minute or two. She felt that she *must* hear the end of the story.

'Ay, that's it,' said Old Grandad, seeming to wake up again. 'But here's the peculiar bit, Missy – no one rang those bells – they rang theirselves!'

Diana gave a little shiver. 'That's what the woman at the Hall said,' she remembered. 'She said the bells rang themselves when Hugh Dourley's son was killed one night – and ever since then they rang themselves when enemies came. And as the wolves were enemies of the little village, I suppose it was right for the bells to ring themselves again! How very weird!'

'Have they rung at other times?' asked Snubby, who was very thrilled by all this.

'Oh, yes – there was the time when the outlaws came creeping up at night,' said Old Grandad. 'And the day when soldiers came to take old Dourley off to prison – that were in my own Grandad's time. Many's the time he's told me that tale. Out rang the bells, all of a sudden, and old James Dourley escaped down the secret passage.'

'The secret passage – the very one we saw yesterday!' said Roger. 'It can't possibly have a blind end then.'

'The soldiers went after him,' went on the old man.

'Down the passage they went, climbing in one after another – but he got away.'

'Where does the passage go to?' asked Roger, getting quite worked up with all these old stories.

'You ask Mother Barlow,' said the old man, and he gave his curious high chuckle again. 'She knows all right.'

The children looked at one another, puzzled.

'But – you said Mother Barlow lived in the time when there were wolves,' said Diana. 'She's not alive now.'

'But she'm there all right,' said Old Grandad. 'In her old cottage. *She* knows, I tell you. Ah, she knows. Old Grandad doesn't give away too many secrets.'

This was most exasperating. The old man must be wandering in his mind, Diana thought. Perhaps he was tired out with all his talking, and was muddling up past and present.

'Don't *you* know where the secret passage goes to?' asked Diana, trying again. 'Does it go to the cellars of Ring O' Bells Hall? Or does it go to–'

'It goes to Mother Barlow,' said the old man obstinately. 'That's where it went when I was a boy. Me and Jim, my brother, we went down there once – and we found some old books.'

'Old books!' said Snubby excited. 'I say – have you still got them?'

'Where did you find them – in the passage – or at Mother Barlow's?' asked Roger, feeling that the old man was getting muddled.

'Down in the passage,' whispered the old man, as if this were a secret. 'There was a little old cupboard there – hidden away – and me and Jim, we opened it. There were books and papers there – and a little old carved box – and I misremember what else.'

'Did you take them?' asked Snubby, after a pause. 'They weren't really yours, so I suppose you didn't.'

46

The old man took another long look back into the past. He began to mumble excitedly.

'Wasn't Jim and me of the Dourley family? Wasn't we Dourleys ourselves, even though we lived in a little cottage, and not at Ring O'Bells Hall? Who knew about them old things? They weren't no value. We thought mebbe some old Dourley had hidden them there long since – and we was Dourleys too, so why shouldn't we have them?'

The children could think of many reasons why the old man and his brother should not have had them, but they said nothing. What they really wanted to know was – were these old treasures still in existence!

Diana spoke to the mumbling old fellow, who now seemed to have got quite lost in the past. She spoke very gently, as if he were a child.

'Old Grandad – don't worry yourself about all this. You took the things, and brought them back. Have you still got them?'

'Aye, we took them back,' said Old Grandad, and a gleam came into his watery eyes. 'Jimmy had the box and I had the books.'

'What were the books about?' asked Roger.

The old fellow snorted. 'How was I to know? I couldn't read. I never did have no learning, but I wasn't any the worse for that.'

This was disappointing. Diana tried again.

'What happened to the books, Grandad? Have you still got them?'

'You ask my granddaughter,' said Old Grandad. 'She've got all my things now. But what's the use of them old books – she've burnt them long ago, no doubt!'

'Grandad, *do* tell us exactly where the secret passage goes,' begged Snubby.

47

The old man scowled at him so ferociously that Snubby drew back in alarm.

'Me and Jim got thrashed for going there,' he said. 'We boasted about it, see – and Mr Paul Dourley, who had the Hall then, he took us and he thrashed us till we yelled for mercy. He said if we told what we knew about it, he'd have us sent away from Ring O' Bells village, sent right away to a foreign country where we'd work as slaves. So Jim and me, we held our tongues. I'm not talking no more about it. You might get summat done to me, you might. Who be you, anyways?'

His voice rose, and he half got out of his chair.

'Why – you know who we are,' said Diana, scared. 'We're just three children. Your granddaughter told you our names and everything. We wouldn't do anything to hurt or harm you.'

But the old man was now so wrapped up in the past that he could no longer place the children in the present. He peered at them, as he sank back in his chair again.

'Who be you? Strangers come to pester me, and get my secrets! Prying and poking and worriting me!'

His voice rose high, and his granddaughter, Mother Hubbard, heard it. She came hurrying over.

'Now, now, Grandad – don't you go exciting yourself! Don't look so scared, children. He's been telling you some of his old tales, hasn't he? He always gets excited then.'

'He thought we were trying to pester him and pry secrets out of him,' said Diana, almost in tears. 'But we were just very interested, that's all.'

'Of course you were,' said Mother Hubbard. 'Now don't you worry. Grandad didn't always do right in his time – he's got a guilty conscience sometimes, poor old man – and when it begins to work, he gets afraid. He'll soon forget!'

She tucked the old man back into his cushions, and led the three children into the house. They looked round, wondering if they would see any old books. They didn't quite like to ask just then, after having upset the old grandfather.

'I must go back to the old man,' Mother Hubbard said, taking them to the little front door. 'You come along again whenever you like. You'll be welcome!'

Chapter Eight

A Morning in the Village

The children wandered off down the road, feeling rather bemused with all they had heard. They came to Ring O' Bells Hall, the two dogs racing round them in delight. They had gone nearly mad at being untied at last, though Mother Hubbard once more supplied them with bones to gnaw and keep them quiet.

They stood still and looked at the old stone mansion.

'I shouldn't have liked to live there,' said Diana.

'Those small windows, the dim light inside, the stone floors and walls, so very cold – ugh! It must have been a very uncomfortable place to live in.'

'And never knowing if the bells were going to ring out by themselves!' said Snubby. 'I should have been scared stiff. How *did* the bells ring by themselves? Who rang them? I mean – bells can't *really* ring themselves.'

'Don't let's talk about it,' said Diana, with a shiver. 'I expect it's all made-up tales, really. Things like that don't happen.'

The woman who acted as guide came out to sweep down the front path, and saw the children standing there.

Loony ran up to her at once and frisked round her in his usual friendly fashion. She swept out at him crossly with her brush.

Loony never could resist a brush. He leapt at it, trying to bite it, quite thinking that the woman was playing some sort of game with him.

Loopy then thought he would join in too, and the

woman got really angry, and half frightened. She hit out with the brush, and the dogs went quite mad with joy.

'Loony! Loopy! Come here!' called Roger at last. The dogs came obediently, and the woman glared at the children.

'Don't you bring them here again,' she said threateningly. 'I'll report you if you do.'

'Who to?' asked Roger. 'Do tell us! Is there a Mr Dourley you can report us to? We'd like to meet him, if so. We want to ask him questions about that secret passage!'

The woman stopped her sweeping and looked at Roger.

'That secret passage? What questions are there to ask? You've seen it, haven't you?'

'Yes – but you said it led to a blind end, and we've heard that it doesn't,' said Roger.

'Well, you heard wrong, then,' said the woman. 'It does. I've seen it myself! It's been walled up now, so it's no longer really a passage. It just comes to a blind end.'

'Oh,' said Roger. That seemed all there was to say. He hadn't thought of that solution. Secret passages were often walled up when they were no longer in use. It *was* quite likely that this one would be too, especially as Ring O'Bells Hall was now a show-place and no longer lived in.

'Do you know where the passage led to?' asked Snubby.

'To nowhere,' said the woman promptly. 'The roof had fallen in, and it was impassable – no one could get through it.'

'But where did it *once* lead to?' persisted Snubby.

'I don't think anyone knows that,' said the woman, beginning to sweep again, keeping a wary eye on Loony and Loopy, who were watching her brush longingly. 'It's not been used for centuries, I should think. Anyway, no one would want to explore the ruined old passage – the roof was likely to fall in at any moment, all the way along.'

'It's a long passage then?' asked Roger. But the woman didn't answer. She merely gave an impatient snort, shook the dust out of her brush, and disappeared into the dark hall behind her.

'She's a bad-tempered creature, isn't she,' said Diana. 'Well – I suppose she's right. The passage got dangerous, was of no use, and was walled up when the Hall was taken over as a show-place. I dare say the old house wasn't lived in for years, and everything was in an awful state. Some society or other must have bought it and opened it to show to tourists or trippers.'

'It's a pretty strange place, I must say, all furnished with old, forgotten things that seem to stand and dream in the rooms,' said Snubby.

The other two stared at him, surprised. 'You've gone all poetical or something,' said Roger.

'No, I haven't,' said Snubby, blushing at the idea of being called poetical. 'That old place seems to have got hold of me somehow. It's mysterious, with its hidden chambers and secret passages and bells that ring themselves. I'd just hate to spend a night there.'

'Well, nobody's asked you to,' said Roger. 'So don't worry!'

'Look – Loony's gone into the Hall!' said Diana suddenly.

'Loony, Loony, Loony!'

Loony came tearing out with a brush in his mouth, looking very pleased with himself indeed.

'You idiot!' said Snubby, and took it from him. It was a small, hard brush, used for stair-carpets and mats.

Snubby took it cautiously back to the front door and peeped inside. There seemed to be no sign of the guide-woman so he tiptoed inside to replace the brush somewhere.

An angry voice made him jump. 'Now then! I can see you, coming in to snoop round without paying! If I have any more bother with you children and your dogs, I'll go straight to the police station and ask them to warn you about your behaviour!'

Snubby saw the woman at the back of the hall looking rather like an angry black witch against the light that trickled in through the slit-window there. He fled, and the others roared with laughter at him, as he came out at top speed, almost falling over the two delighted dogs.

'Heard the bells, or something?' inquired Roger. 'My word – your legs must have got over their jelly-feeling, or they wouldn't have taken you so fast just then. Talk about being jet-propelled!'

'Oh, stop it!' said Snubby crossly. 'Let's go and get some ice creams or something – if they've got any in this old village! They've probably never even heard of them.'

They went on down to the village. Diana began to talk about Old Grandad. 'It's like turning the pages of history to hear him talk,' she said. 'Wasn't it extraordinary, though, the way he mixed everything up – the past and the present – and thought we were people out of the past come to find out his old, old secrets and punish him. Poor old man.'

'Fancy him going down that secret passage and finding those old books and that carved box,' said Snubby. 'I suppose the box has gone long ago – he said his brother took that, didn't he? But it's quite likely that the *books* are still about somewhere.'

'He would probably have been scared in case anyone found out that he'd taken them,' said Roger, 'and he'd have hidden them away for years. Then he probably forgot

53

about them, and his granddaughter found them when she kept house for the old man.'

'And quite likely put them on the rubbish heap,' said Diana. 'Fancy the old fellow not being able to read! How tantalising to have exciting old books like that and not be able to read them!'

'I don't expect we'd be able to, either,' said Roger, making his way to a small village store that appeared to sell everything. 'I expect the words are in that peculiar old writing where all the letter s's are f's.'

'Or maybe in Latin,' said Diana. 'Well, Snubby could translate that all right, couldn't you, Snubby? You're good at Latin, aren't you?'

Snubby gave her a punch. Everyone knew that the remarks about Latin on Snubby's report were most sarcastic. Latin was not Snubby's best subject.

They sat down and had ice creams. They were very good ones too, made of real cream. After that they had glasses of orangeade, and felt much better.

'I'm almost forgetting we've had 'flu now,' said Snubby, sucking up his orangeade through a long straw. 'I feel much more myself.'

'What a pity,' said Roger. 'A little of you goes a long way, Snubby. Too far.'

'Don't be funny,' said Snubby. 'I don't feel well enough yet to punch your head when you make one of your fat-headed remarks – but I soon shall!'

'Woof,' said Loony, putting a paw on Snubby's knee. Snubby looked down. 'What do you want? You don't like orangeade.'

'Maybe he's thirsty,' said the shopwoman, and she put down a dish of water for the dogs. They lapped noisily.

'Oh, thanks!' said Snubby. 'That's nice of you!'

The shop bell rang and somebody came in. Diana nudged Roger.

'Somebody out of a fairy tale,' she whispered. It was a little old woman in an old red cloak. A ragged hood hung down her back.

'Red Riding Hood grown old,' whispered back Roger. Diana nodded in delight. Yes – Red Riding Hood grown old – and maybe still living in the same cottage as in her childhood. It wasn't possible of course – but it pleased Diana to fancy it!

'A pound of butter, please – and an ounce of black pepper – and a bag of flour – and a jar of your own honey,' said the cloaked customer, in a small clear voice. She turned to look at the children as she stood waiting.

She had curious eyes – almost green, Diana thought. Her mouth was the mouth of an old woman, fallen in and toothless, but her eyes were still very bright. Her hair was snow-white and still curly, and she smiled and nodded at the children.

'Good morning,' she said, in her small, rather child-like voice. 'Are you visiting here?'

'Yes,' said Diana politely. 'We're staying with Miss Hannah Pepper. We've had 'flu so that's why we're not back at school yet. Do you know Miss Pepper?'

'Oh yes,' said the old woman. 'I worked for her mother years ago. You tell her you've seen me – she'll remember me all right.'

'I will,' said Diana. 'What is your name?'

'Barlow,' said the old lady. 'Naomi Barlow, and I live out in Ring O' Bells Wood.'

'Barlow!' said all three children at once. They had immediately remembered what Old Grandad had said. 'Ask Mother Barlow!' Could this old woman be the same Mother Barlow he was thinking of?

Before they could make up their minds to ask her, the old lady was away out of the shop with her bag of goods. Diana turned to the shopwoman.

55

'Er – we've heard today of a Mother Barlow,' she said. 'I suppose – I suppose *that* wasn't Mother Barlow, was it?'

The shopwoman laughed. 'Dear me, no – Mother Barlow lived long ago – before my time! She lived where old Naomi lives now – in Ring O' Bells Cottage away out in the wood.'

Chapter Nine

Talk at Tea-Time

The children paid their bill and walked slowly back to Hannah Pepper's cottage. 'Ring O' Bells Cottage away out in the wood!' repeated Diana two or three times. 'This is all getting more like a nursery rhyme place than ever – or a fairy tale!'

'Did you notice the curious greenish eyes that Naomi Barlow had?' asked Roger rather sheepishly. 'Witches have green eyes – or they were supposed to.'

'Don't be silly,' said Snubby. '*She* wasn't anything like a witch – she was a nice old thing, I thought.'

'I didn't say she was a witch, or even *like* one,' said Roger. 'I just pointed out that she had unusual eyes. I'm not idiot enough to believe in witches nowadays.'

'*I* thought she looked exactly what Red Riding Hood would look like when she grew old,' said Diana. 'With that old red cloak and ragged hood. You could imagine Red Riding Hood keeping the cloak for years and years and years.'

'She'd probably grow out of it,' said Snubby, getting rather tired of this conversation about green eyes and witches and cloaks. 'Let's get home quickly. I'm *just* beginning to feel my legs going a bit wobbly again.'

'You and your legs,' said Diana. 'There doesn't look anything wrong with them to me.'

Miss Pepper insisted on their having a rest again that afternoon, though Snubby, whose legs seemed to have made a miraculous recovery, wanted to go and hire a horse for riding over the countryside.

'Well, you can't,' said Miss Pepper. 'You're to have a rest.'

'Couldn't I just have a quarter of an hour's rest and then take Loony for a walk?' asked Snubby. 'He's awfully fat. He *needs* a long walk this afternoon.'

'I agree with you,' said Miss Pepper. 'He's much too fat – and he does need a long walk. I'll take him myself this afternoon, with Loopy – though my name will probably be Dotty, when I come back – I shall certainly be driven crazy with two mad dogs capering round me.'

'Ha ha – joke,' said Snubby automatically. He didn't think much of Miss Pepper's jokes. 'No, Miss Pepper – I'd rather have Loony on my bed with me, thank you. You can take Loopy.'

'Thank you very much,' said Miss Pepper. 'Now *will* you go upstairs at once and do as you're told? I warn you that if you start being awkward, I shall go back to an old punishment of mine, and you won't like it.'

'What's that?' asked Snubby, with great interest. 'I'm sure I shouldn't mind your punishments very much, Miss Pepper.'

'Right,' said Miss Pepper. 'We'll try this one then – no jam or cake at tea – only bread and butter.'

This didn't sound so good. Snubby hastily went up the stairs, with Loony at his heels. He felt sure he would be far too hungry at tea-time to relish a silly punishment like that.

He was more tired than he knew, and slept solidly till tea-time, with Loony stretched over his legs, sleeping too. Loopy could not imagine where Loony disappeared to in the afternoons and, after hunting vainly for him in all kinds of unlikely places, including the coal-hole, he went off happily with Miss Pepper for a walk.

Snubby was very glad that Miss Pepper said nothing about his having no jam or cake at tea, when he sat down at tea-time feeling extraordinarily hungry after his long sleep.

'Hot scones!' he said, touching the warm dish. 'Goody! Home-made butter and home-made honey! Couldn't be better. And what's that over there? New currant-bread? Oh, I say – whatever shall I begin on first?'

'Don't sound so greedy, Snubby,' said Diana, helping herself to a scone. 'And don't gobble. You've got plenty of time before you reach the cake stage.'

'Shut up,' said Snubby. '*You* can teach me about gobbling any time!'

Miss Hannah looked across at Miss Pepper, and gave her a small smile. 'They're rapidly recovering from the 'flu,' she said.

'They are,' said Miss Pepper. 'Snubby, will you tell Loony to remove himself from my feet. I think he's under the impression that he's sitting on yours, and he's really very heavy.'

Loony removed himself, and Loopy immediately took his place. Miss Pepper put up with it. She didn't like to ask Hannah to tell Loopy to remove *himself*. The dogs always seemed to play this kind of 'musical chairs' at meal times.

'I wonder if old Barney will come quickly,' said Snubby. 'I wonder if he's got our letter yet.'

'Of course he hasn't,' said Diana. 'We only posted it this morning.'

'Did we really?' said Snubby, astonished. 'You know, this holiday's beginning to act like all holidays – time seems to get all muddled up – and then, whoosh – the whole holiday's gone before you've even got it by the tail.'

'Don't talk such nonsense, Snubby,' said Miss Pepper – but Diana and Roger knew exactly what Snubby meant.

'Miss Hannah,' said Diana, remembering the green-eyed old woman in the village shop, 'do you know an old lady called Naomi Barlow?'

'Dear me, yes,' said Miss Hannah. 'She worked for my dear old mother years ago – and a very good worker she was too. I remember her from when I was a small girl. She must be quite old now.'

'She lives in Ring O' Bells Cottage,' said Roger.

'Yes,' said Miss Pepper suddenly. 'That's the little cottage in the woods – the one I always thought must belong to Red Riding Hood.'

'Old Naomi Barlow has a red cloak and hood,' said Diana. 'She probably had them when she was much younger and you might have seen her. Miss Pepper. I expect that's what made you think of Red Riding Hood Cottage.'

'Do you know anything about old Mother Barlow who used to live in the same cottage years and years ago?' asked Roger.

'No,' said Miss Hannah. 'I've just heard the name somewhere, that's all. How did you hear about her?'

'We talked to Old Grandad this morning,' said Diana. 'You know – Mother Hubbard's grandfather.'

'Mother Hubbard?' said Miss Hannah, surprised. 'Whoever is she?'

'Well, that mayn't be her right name,' said Roger, 'but she lives at Hubbard Cottage and she *looks* exactly like Mother Hubbard. She's got a very old grandfather – he says he's over a hundred years old – but he looks more like two hundred to me.'

'Don't be absurd, Roger,' said Miss Pepper. 'I know who you mean, of course. I don't know his real name – everyone calls him Old Grandad.'

'His real name is Hugh Dourley and he's related in some way to the old Dourleys who used to live in Ring O' Bells Hall,' said Diana. '*He* told us about Mother

60

Barlow. He said she knew all about the secret passage under Ring O' Bells Hall.'

Miss Pepper looked bewildered – but her cousin followed what Diana meant. 'What a lot you seem to have found out in a day or two!' she said. 'I do remember a bit more about old Mother Barlow now. She must have lived about eighty or ninety years ago – when Old Grandad was a bit of a boy.'

'He *could* have known her then,' said Diana. 'Oh, what a pity she's not alive now – she could have told us all the secrets of Ring O' Bells Hall. Perhaps she even knew who it is that rings the bells to warn the village of danger!'

'Oh, that's an old, old story, almost a legend,' said Miss Hannah. 'The bells haven't rung during *my* lifetime! And you may be sure that if ever they did ring, they were rung by human' hands. It was people like old Mother Barlow who put about these peculiar old stories. She was supposed to be a witch.'

'Was she *really*?' asked Diana. 'Oh, Miss Hannah! Then no wonder Naomi Barlow's got green eyes – she takes after Mother Barlow, the witch!'

'Don't take all this too seriously,' said Miss Pepper. 'These are only old tales and legends, with possibly no truth in them at all. Mother Barlow was probably a kindly old woman, who knew a good bit about herbs and the roots of plants, and could make medicines and ointments to cure all kinds of ills. That would be quite enough to make her a witch in the eyes of the ignorant village people!'

'I do like this place,' said Diana. 'I really do like places that are old and full of long-ago tales. Bits of real history are wrapped up in them, and it's so exciting to unwrap them and discover what they are.'

'As for Old Grandad, he's like a real live history book,'

said Roger. 'Why, he even told us a tale about wolves coming to Ring O' Bells Village!'

'That may be quite true,' said Miss Hannah. 'There is a place outside the village called Wolfwick – only a glen now with a cottage or two – where the wolves were supposed to gather in winter time.'

'I wish we could wake up one morning and find ourselves back in the past,' sighed Diana. 'Just to see what it was like. We might see Mother Barlow going by the window on her way to work.'

'And we'd see a sprightly youth with his brother, capering by to go to work in the fields,' said Roger with a grin.

'Who would they be?' asked Diana.

'Old Grandad and his brother Jim,' said Roger. 'I know it's impossible to think of Old Grandad ever being young, but he must have been.'

'And we might hear the bells ringing in Ring O' Bells Hall one night,' said Snubby. 'And if we could see into the old place, it would be full of the old Dourleys who lived there – children like us, but dressed differently.'

'And their dogs,' said Roger. 'Spaniels like Loony and Loopy, I expect. They were used a lot for country sport.'

Loony and Loopy had got up immediately on hearing their names. They came from under the table, wagging their tails eagerly, putting heavy paws up on Snubby and Roger.

'Are you tired of this silly conversation?' said Snubby, pulling Loony's long ears.

'We seem to have sat here a long time,' said Miss Pepper, pushing her chair back. 'Have you all finished?'

'Well, there's nothing left to eat,' said Snubby. And he was right. Every plate was empty, the whole of the currant-loaf was gone, and the big new fruitcake had disappeared too.

'I should think you'll be able to last till breakfast-time

now,' said Miss Pepper hard-heartedly, and was quite surprised at the chorus of, 'No, Miss Pepper, *no*!'

Chapter Ten

Barney Starts on a Journey

Next day the children went off to the riding stables and asked for horses to hack round the countryside. The owner was a youngish woman with a face so like a horse that it quite astonished the children.

She wore her hair tied down at the back of her neck like a horse's tail, and had a laugh like the whinny of a horse. But she was very nice indeed, and soon sized up the children's ability.

'You can have Tom Tit Tot,' she said to Snubby, who wasn't as big as the other two. 'And let me warn you, he stands no nonsense, so don't play the fool with him.'

He was a good little pony, sturdy, with white socks and a star on his forehead. Snubby liked him.

Diana had a quiet horse called Lady, and Roger had a fine-looking one called Heyho. The children had put on jodhpurs, yellow jerseys and riding coats – but they were far too hot, and left their coats hanging up on nails in the stables.

They walked their horses through the gate and into the road. 'Take the road up the hill and down through Ring O' Bells Wood,' said the riding mistress, when she saw them off. 'It's a beautiful ride, and good going for the horses.'

It was a most magnificent day. Birds sang joyously, lambs, fat and frisky, leapt about the hillside, the haw-thorn was out everywhere like snow-drifts on the hedges. The trees were in new leaf, tender and green, and daisies sprinkled the grass all around.

'Oh Maytime, fold thy fleeting wing,
And let it be forever spring!'

sang Diana, as she cantered over a daisy-strewn path,
away up the hill.

They had a good gallop that morning. The horses were
fresh and happy, and the children were good horsemen.
They went almost to the top of the hill, which was long,
but not very steep and enjoyed the magnificent view
below.

'There's Ring O' Bells Village,' said Diana, pointing
with her whip. 'And look – aren't those the towers of
Ring O' Bells Hall – one square and one round, peeping
above the trees?'

'Yes – and there's the church,' said Snubby. 'Its spire
is sticking right up, not far from the Hall. Can we see
Miss Hannah's house from here?'

They couldn't. The wood stretched between them and
the house and hid it. It was a big wood, full of beech and
oak, some of the trees very tall and spreading.

'Look – there's a thin thread of blue smoke rising up
from that corner of the wood over there,' said Snubby
pointing. 'There must be a house in the wood.'

'Well, we know there is,' said Roger. 'Ring O' Bells
Cottage is there – where Naomi Barlow lives.'

'Oh, of course!' said Snubby. 'It's really not very far
from Ring O' Bells Hall, is it, tucked away in that corner
of the wood?'

'It's much farther than it looks,' said Diana. 'Can't you
picture old Mother Barlow down there in the cottage,
perhaps a hundred years ago, bending over her black iron
pot, boiling up all kinds of herbs and roots and things?
Perhaps the people of Ring O' Bells Hall bought their
physics from her – their ointments and medicines and
lotions.'

'A green-eyed witch,' said Roger. 'All the books say that witches or anyone distantly related to the Little Folk have green eyes. I'm sure Naomi's old grandmother, or whoever she was, was a witch, and that's why Naomi has green eyes.'

The horses stamped impatiently, and Loony and Loopy appeared from the rabbit holes they had been excitedly examining.

'Come on,' said Snubby. 'We sound a bit cracked when we talk like this. We none of us really believe it!'

But in their secret hearts they wondered if there *was* some truth in the old, old stories, and if bits of that truth were not still hidden here and there in this beautiful, ancient countryside. Diana, especially, wanted to believe it – it was romantic and exciting and mysterious.

They rode back through Ring O' Bells Wood. The path was broad, and the horses knew it well. Occasionally the children had to dodge twigs and low branches by bending this way and that. The wood was rather silent, and although sunshine came in here and there through the branches of the trees, their way seemed dim and shadowy.

'I wonder if we pass Ring O' Bells Cottage,' said Diana. 'It must be somewhere near here.'

'I can see smoke from a chimney, anyway,' said Snubby. 'It must be quite near. We shall pass it!'

But they didn't. A little path ran off the main path, and wound away between the trees. That must be the way to the cottage. Diana glanced at her watch.

'We oughtn't to stop and have a look at the cottage today,' she said regretfully. 'It's getting so late and we promised to have the horses back by half-past twelve. Anyway, it's a very narrow path for horses. We'd better bring the dogs up here for a walk one day, and have a good look at the old place.'

'Right,' said Roger, turning his horse down the broad

path. 'Come on. There's a good clearing there – we'll gallop!'

It was a good ride, and all three enjoyed it very much. The horses enjoyed it too, and the two dogs trotted home happily, their long pink tongues curling out of their mouths.

What a lunch the children ate! Miss Hannah looked on, quite dismayed, as they demolished a huge stew and an even huger treacle pudding.

'Becky, we can't let them go riding every morning if this is how it makes them eat!' she said comically.

'You can always do plenty more potatoes,' said Diana.

'I did you four each as it was,' said Miss Hannah. 'Well, well – you'll certainly feel better after today!'

They were tired that night, though. They only had a very short rest that afternoon, and by the time eight o'clock came not one of them could keep his eyes open. Even the dogs, tired out by their long walk, lay motionless on the hearth-rug, Loopy's head resting on Loony's black body. They were very fond of one another.

As they undressed, the two boys wondered about Barney. Had he got their letter yet? Would he, by any chance, arrive the next day? What fun if he did!

'Di!' called Snubby through the door. 'We're talking about Barney. He might come tomorrow, if he's got our letter.'

'Well, that's the very earliest he could arrive!' said Diana, getting into bed. 'We'll look out for him. Good old Barney. I wonder what Loopy will say to Miranda. He's never seen her. I should think old Loony will go mad with joy.'

Barney *was* on his way! He had got Diana's letter that very morning, and had read it with delight. He had no idea where Ring O' Bells Village was, of course. He had been sleeping in a caravan lent to him by one of the men he knew, and all he had to do was to tidy it up, and return the key to the owner. Then he was ready to leave.

Barney travelled light. All his possessions were in a big red handkerchief, tied up in a knot, and either slung over his shoulder on the end of a stick, or carried knotted about his arm.

Miranda, of course, travelled on one or other of his shoulders! She sat there, a little bright-eyed creature, with an old, wizened-looking face, and a host of youthful ways. She was as mad and playful as a kitten.

'Now, Miranda, we're off on our travels again,' Barney said to her, as they set off together. 'You've had a mighty fine time lately – bossing all the other monkeys and pretending you're Princess Miranda, too high and mighty to do any performing in the ring!'

Miranda chattered back at him gaily. Barney listened seriously as if he understood every word. He certainly answered her as if he had!

'Well, I'm glad to hear you enjoyed yourself so much. Now who do you think we're going to see? Guess!'

Miranda bounced up and down on his shoulder, chattering again.

'Quite right, Miranda! We *are* going to see Diana, Roger and Snubby,' said Barney. 'And don't forget Loony!'

Most excited this time, Miranda gave another bounce or two. She recognised Loony's name, and a picture of the little black spaniel flashed into her monkey mind. She chattered excitedly, and nibbled Barney's ear.

'Now then, now then,' said Barney. 'Careful with that ear. You've already taken the edge off it.'

People turned and smiled as they saw the big, loose-limbed boy walking down the road, with the little monkey on his shoulder. Barney was very striking to look at, with his brilliant blue eyes set in his brown face. His hair was thick, the colour of ripe corn, and he looked the picture of health.

He took Diana's letter from his pocket, and looked at the address. He thought he had better try and make for the big town of Lillinghame, rather than for the village of Ring O' Bells. It wasn't likely that any lorry or van would be going to that little village, but one might go to Lillinghame, or near it.

He stood by the roadside, with Miranda on his shoulder, thumbing passing lorries. At last one stopped and the man beckoned him up to the seat beside him.

'That a monkey?' he said. 'Is she tame?'

'Oh yes,' said Barney. 'Salute this kind gentleman, Miranda.'

Miranda saluted smartly, bringing her tiny paw up to her forehead and down again. The man laughed.

'Well, I've given many people a lift, but never a monkey. This will be something to tell my little boy at home tonight. Where do you want to go to, mate?'

'Do you know Lillinghame?' asked Barney.

'Never heard of it,' said the driver disappointingly. 'Where is it?'

'It's in the county of Somerset,' said Barney, looking at Diana's letter. The man whistled.

'That's a long way, chum. You won't get there before tomorrow, unless you're lucky. I'm going about fifty miles on your way, then I turn off. You'll have to pick up another lorry then, going in your direction.'

'Right. Thanks,' said Barney, and off they went on the first stage of his long journey to Ring O' Bells.

Chapter Eleven

Hitch-Hiking all the Way

Barney and Miranda enjoyed the ride. They both liked
the fresh air in their faces, and Miranda enjoyed the
fussing and petting she got whenever the lorry stopped,
and the driver had a minute to spare. He was very proud
when she actually went to sit on his shoulder whilst he
drove.

'She's got her paw down my neck, under my collar,' he
said to Barney. 'I say – I suppose you wouldn't sell her,
would you?'

'No, I wouldn't,' said Barney at once. 'For one thing
I'm too fond of her – and for another she'd pine away
and die if she left me.'

He hopped down after they had gone about fifty miles,
and the driver rattled on, waving goodbye to him and
Miranda, quite sorry to part from them both. Barney
went to a roadside café to get something to eat, and to
ask where was the best place to wait for lorries to thumb.

'Wait here, mate,' said the café owner, polishing his
cups till they shone. 'This is a good pull-up for lorries –
there'll be a lot along presently. Where do you want to
go?'

'To Lillinghame in Somerset,' said Barney.

'You're a long way from there,' said the man. 'Let's
see now – you want to take the Biddlington road – and
get a lorry to drop you off at Biddlington. Then, if you're
lucky you'll get a ride right into Somerset, and be able to
pick up another lorry to Lillinghame.'

Lorries drove in soon after that, and the men got down

for snacks and a cup of coffee. The café owner introduced Barney and Miranda, and inquired whether anyone could take them on their way.

'I'm going that way,' volunteered a middle-aged driver, 'but I don't know as I can do with monkeys sitting beside me. I never did take to them.'

'Can I sit at the back then, out of your way?' asked Barney, anxious not to lose the lift. So it was agreed that he should sit at the back among the crates that the lorry was carrying.

It was very uncomfortable indeed. The floor of the van was hard, and the crates were even harder, the van shook as it rattled over the roads at a good speed, and poor Barney began to feel very bruised indeed. He was thankful when the van slowed down and the driver yelled to him.

'Better get down here, lad. I'll be taking you out of your way if you go any farther with me.'

Barney shouted his thanks and jumped down quickly with Miranda. The van rattled away, leaving him standing on a broad deserted road.

His luck was not so good after that. Not many lorries came by, and only a few private cars, which took no notice of him. Nobody wanted a monkey in a car!

Barney trudged on, mile after mile, thumbing each lorry or van that passed. He came to a small town and had something to eat, for he was getting very hungry. He bought Miranda a banana and some raisins. She loved raisins and spent a most enjoyable time picking the pips out of each before eating them.

The only thing was that she took it into her head to poke the pips down Barney's neck! 'Stop it!' said Barney in disgust. 'Miranda, I'm surprised at you – nasty, sticky, messy pips like that! I'll take your raisins away if you do that any more.'

Miranda stopped putting the pips down his neck, and spat them into the road instead. Barney laughed and went to stand at a good corner for thumbing traffic.

Nobody stopped for him until an enormous removal van came slowly by. Barney thumbed it hopefully. The two men sitting in front took no notice, but then one of them suddenly caught sight of Miranda on Barney's shoulder.

He nudged his companion, and the big van stopped.

'That a monkey you've got, mate?' yelled the driver.

'Yes!' yelled back Barney, and went to the front of the van.

'You go at the back of the van then, and tell Alf,' said the driver, with a broad grin. 'He's daft on monkeys. He'll let you go into the van and sit with him, if you'll let him play with your monkey.'

This was a bit of luck. Barney ran to the back of the van. A small man, with moustache rather like a walrus's was already looking out to see why the removal van had stopped so suddenly. When he saw Barney with Miranda he grinned in delight.

'They told you to come along and look for me, didn't they?' he said, nodding his head towards the front of the van. 'They know I'm cracked about monkeys. Come along in, lad, and make yourself comfortable. Where do you want to go to?'

Barney told him. The little man took down a map and had a look at it. He put a dirty fingernail on a certain spot and handed it to Barney. He held out his arms to Miranda, and the little creature leapt straight into them. Barney was surprised.

'They all know me,' said the small man, winking at Barney. 'I go to the Zoo whenever I'm back in London, and you should see the monkeys when they spot me coming along. They all crowd to one side of the cage, the nearest they can get to me, and put their tiny hands through the bars for their titbits. Talk about dogs! Give me a monkey every time! As for cats, you can have the lot. Now a monkey is–'

He went on chattering without a pause, and soon Miranda began chattering too. Barney looked up in amusement. The two of them looked distinctly alike! The man had a little wizened face, with monkey eyes, and his moustache looked like thick whiskers. He was enjoying himself thoroughly.

Barney had a much more comfortable journey this time. The van was full of furniture, and he and the little man reclined at their ease in big soft arm-chairs whose springs gave to every bump on the road. Barney felt as if he could go to sleep at any moment!

He had looked at the map, which he didn't understand at all. He knew all he needed to know – that he had to get off at the third big town, and then see whether he could get a lift from there to Lillinghame. He could walk after that.

The little monkey-faced man was almost in tears at having to part with Miranda when the van drew up at the town where Barney had to get out. Miranda clung to him as if she too hated to part with him, but when she saw Barney stepping down from the van, she was on his shoulder with one enormous bound. She waved to the disconsolate little man.

'Well, you certainly gave him a treat, and got us a welcome lift,' said Barney to Miranda, as he waited at the corner for another lorry to come by. It was getting rather dark by this time. Barney began to wonder if he would get to Ring O' Bells Village in time to see the children.

It was quite dark when a small, closed van came by. As it passed a lamp-post Barney saw the name on it.

'PIGGOTT, ELECTRICIAN.' He stepped out and thumbed it.

It accelerated at once, swerved past him and went on. Barney was used to this sort of thing and stepped back to the pavement. Then he saw that the van had stopped some way down the road. He wondered why. Perhaps it had stopped for him, after all?

He went to see. He soon saw that the van had a puncture in one of the front wheels. The driver was already out of his seat and looking at it.

'Bad luck, mate,' said Barney, going up. 'Want any help? That was a pretty sudden puncture.'

'This wheel's been a bit of a nuisance lately,' said the man. He was short and plump, but that was all that Barney could make out in the dark. 'Do you know anything about changing a wheel? I don't want to get my hands filthy, and all the garages will be shut by now. I'll make it worth your while if you can change this wheel for me.'

'Yes – I know how to change wheels,' said Barney. 'And if you'd give me a lift to Lillinghame, if you're going there, sir, that'd be payment enough. I just want a lift, that's all.'

The man hesitated. He struck a match and looked at Barney as if he wondered whether he might be taking on a rogue or a ruffian for a lift. When he saw that Barney was only a boy, he looked relieved. 'Right,' he said. 'You change my wheel and I'll take you to Lillinghame. I go right through it.'

Barney was pleased. He set to work, whilst Miranda sat on the roof of the van and watched. She disappeared after a while, and the man looked round for her.

'Where's that monkey of yours?' he asked. 'I don't want her in my van.'

'Miranda!' called Barney. There was a scuffle from

inside the van, and then Miranda's face appeared at a small open window in front of the van, just by the driver's seat.

'She went inside!' exclaimed the man. 'Get her out quick!'

'She won't do any harm to anything, sir,' said Barney. Miranda had now disappeared again inside the van. She was very inquisitive and liked to explore and examine any strange place as thoroughly as possible.

Suddenly there was an agonised shriek from her inside the van. Barney snatched up a torch the man had lent him, and thrust it inside the opening in the front of the van. He was just in time to see something white moving quickly at the bottom of the van. Miranda was crouched at the back, squealing in fright.

Barney watched to see if the moving white thing appeared again, but he could see nothing but boxes and sacks. Then he felt himself roughly pulled away and the torch snatched from his hand.

The driver shouted at him. 'Come away from there, you and your monkey. Don't mess about with my goods.'

'All right, all right,' said Barney, surprised at all the excitement. 'Here, Miranda, what's frightened you?'

The monkey had now climbed out, and had scrambled on to Barney's shoulder, trembling. Something had obviously given her a fright.

'Shall I finish changing the wheel, sir?' asked Barney. 'Sorry my monkey got inside. She's always so inquisitive.'

The man hesitated, then spoke roughly. 'All right – finish the wheel, but buck up about it. I don't want to be all night on the road!'

Chapter Twelve

Journey's End

Barney finished changing the wheel in silence, with Miranda clinging tightly to his shoulder, still very scared. The boy was remembering the white moving thing he had seen in the van. What was it? It was something that had frightened Miranda very much, that was plain. Was it something alive, or what?

'Thanks,' said the man, when Barney had finished. 'Here's some money. I won't give you a lift after all. I've changed my mind.'

'Oh no, you haven't,' said Barney, and he slipped quickly into the seat beside the driver. 'A bargain is a bargain. I don't want money. I want a lift. Now don't try to turn me off my seat, or my monkey will fly at you. She can bite hard.'

The man said something under his breath, stood still for a moment and then climbed up into his own seat. He let in the clutch, and away they went into the night, the van's strong lights raking the road in front of them.

Neither Barney nor the man said a word. Miranda made no sound, but clung to Barney tightly. She didn't like this man beside him.

'Here's Lillinghame,' said the man at last, and stopped. He said no more at all, but watched Barney get down. Barney looked up in the darkness into the white blur of the man's face.

'Thanks,' he said. 'Tell me one thing before I go. What have you got in your van that frightened my monkey so much?'

'Pah!' said the man, fiercely and angrily, and drove off so suddenly that Barney almost fell to the ground. He laughed and patted Miranda.

'Whatever's in that van is a mystery,' he said. 'And if you could talk really *properly*, Miranda, you could tell me what it was. Nasty little fellow, wasn't he?'

Barney walked on until he came to a signpost. He heaved a sigh of relief, because on it, lighted now by the moon which had sailed out from behind a cloud, was the name he wanted – RING O' BELLS!

'Good,' said Barney. 'I haven't done so badly to come all the way here in one day. The thing is – it's too late to find where Roger and the others are now – so we'll just walk into Ring O' Bells, Miranda, and see if we can find somewhere to sleep.'

As he walked down the road, the moon sailed into great black clouds that were coming up from the west. Soon rain fell, and Barney pulled up his coat collar. He debated whether to shelter under a hedge or not, but decided to go on. The rain might not last long.

He trudged on, with Miranda now tucked under his coat. She hated the rain. He came to another signpost at a fork in the road. 'RING O'BELLS two miles.'

That didn't seem far to Barney. The rain was now only a drizzle, so on he went, whistling very softly. Tomorrow he would see his friends. He hadn't seen them for weeks and weeks. It would be good to meet them all again.

He walked down the road and along lanes, past small cottages and one or two farmhouses. Then after passing into Ring O' Bells Village, which was now silent and dark with not a light to be seen, Barney stood still and debated with himself.

Where now? The rain had begun to pour again, and he didn't somehow fancy a night under a hedge. He might

77

find a haystack and burrow into that. So on he went, bending his head to the pelting rain.

He came to a great building, its black shadow making the night even darker. He wondered what it was. If it was a church, perhaps he could creep into the porch and sleep there out of the rain. He walked cautiously up the flagged path, and then stopped.

He could hear voices – low voices. Where were they? Barney slipped into the shadow of a bush. He waited. Then he heard a door closing very quietly, and some one came up the flagged path in soft-soled shoes. Then someone went to the gate – and then, to Barney's amazement, he heard a car starting up outside!

He hadn't noticed any car outside. It must have been driven well into the shadow of the hedge, or he would surely have seen it. He ran on tiptoe to the gate. Someone stood there, lighting a cigarette, unaware that there was anyone watching nearby. As the match flared up, Barney recognised him!

'It's the man who gave me a lift to Lillinghame – the man whose wheel I changed for him!' he thought. 'Short and plump – and with very black eyebrows and jutting chin. I caught sight of his face when we passed a lamp-post during the drive. I wish I'd taken more notice of him now. What's he up to?'

Barney watched the little van disappear up the road, its red light getting fainter and fainter. He wondered if he ought to have taken the number, but the rear light was far too dim to allow him to read anything on the back of the car.

He turned back to the building behind him and wondered what it was. It couldn't be a church, he thought. Was it a private house?

The rain stopped. The moon came out again, and Barney stepped quickly into shadow. Then he caught sight of a big notice set up near the front door. He went on tiptoe towards it.

He read it carefully. Well! After all, the building was only an old show-place – a museum or something, Barney thought. He wondered if he could shelter inside somewhere. He was wet, and would like to take off his coat.

There must be someone inside, surely, because he had heard voices – and yet, only one man had gone to the car. So perhaps he had better not try to get in. He might be arrested as a thief, if he were found.

Barney had no sooner thought this than he heard the sound of cautious footsteps inside the front door, near the noticeboard. He slipped round to the side of the house. He heard the door open, and then it was shut very quietly. Someone came down the flagged path, keeping to the shadowed side.

The someone gave a little cough, and Barney stiffened in surprise. That was a woman's cough! Whatever could a *woman* be doing wandering about in the darkness like this? The figure soon disappeared into the shadows of the lane, and then there was silence.

Barney went to the front door and tried it. Locked, of course. He went all round the place, but found every window locked or shuttered.

The moon shone down through one window as he peered inside. 'Gracious! It's all furnished – it's not empty, or full of cases and things like museums usually are,' said Barney, in surprise. 'I wish I could get into *this* room – I could sleep very comfortably on that old sofa!'

Ivy grew very thickly indeed on one wall. Barney looked up at the thick green screen and noticed a window on the first floor. It *looked* as if it might be open.

He tried his weight on the ivy stems. They were as thick as small trunks, and held his weight easily. So up he went like a cat, testing each ivy stem as he climbed.

Miranda climbed beside him, flinging herself up and down the ivy in a way that Barney very much envied.

He got to the window and found that he was right. It was a small casement window, and because the fastening was broken, it could not be shut. It had swung open and Barney saw that he could easily get inside, once he had got astride the windowsill.

He pulled himself up. Miranda shot up to his shoulder at once. She had seen the half-open window and had guessed Barney was going to enter there. It wasn't long before they were both in the old room behind the open window.

The moon went in and Barney stood still in the darkness. He waited till the moon came out again and then saw that he was in an old-fashioned bedroom. An enormous four-poster bed stood in the middle of the room, almost shut in by side-hangings that were slightly pulled back with tarnished gilt girdles.

Barney tiptoed to the door and opened it. He found himself on a gallery that ran round a great room below, overlooking it. All was silence. Not even a mouse pattered across the floor.

Barney found the stairs and went down. They were shallow stairs that swept down in a curve, right into the big room below. Smaller rooms opened off it. Barney peeped cautiously into each, but there was nobody there, and not a sound to be heard. It did seem quite safe to sleep upstairs in that great four-poster!

A screech made him jump, and Miranda gibbered in fright. But it was only a barn owl outside, screeching to frighten the fieldmice into sudden movement, so that it could see them and pounce.

Barney decided to go upstairs again. He was damp and very tired. He didn't think it would matter if he slept on that great bed. He would take off his shoes and his wet coat. Perhaps there would be something up there that he could wrap himself in.

He went up the wide stairs, and came to the gallery again. He found the bedroom through whose window he had climbed. He looked around in the moonlight for something to wrap round himself.

There was an old table in one corner, covered by a tablecloth of some kind. Barney couldn't see what colour it was or what it was made of. He fingered it, and it felt thick and warm. He pulled it off, took off his coat, and wrapped himself round in the tablecloth. It certainly was nice and cosy!

Miranda tucked herself into its folds, glad to think they were going to bed. She was tired out with her long and exciting day.

Barney slid his shoes off his feet. He felt his socks. Blow, they had holes in them already – just as he wanted to visit his friends too. Well, perhaps he had better wear shoes and no socks, then the holes wouldn't be noticed!

He got on to the bed. It was high, rather hard, and not really very comfortable, but it was bliss to poor, tired Barney. Dragging the tablecloth closely round him, he put his head on the pillow and immediately fell asleep.

Not very far away, at Miss Hannah's house, Diana was lying awake, wondering if Barney would come the next day. Little did she know that at that very moment he was fast asleep in the middle of the old four-poster bed in the best bedroom of Ring O' Bells Hall!

Yes – Ring O' Bells Hall. That was where Barney had ended up for the night. Wake up early, Barney, or you'll be discovered – and then what trouble you'll be getting into!

Chapter Thirteen

Up in the Bell-Tower

Fortunately for Barney he did awake quite early the next morning. The sun shone directly into the window, and a bright beam rested on his face. It woke him, and he sat up blinking in the yellow sunlight, wondering wherever in the world he was.

He soon remembered. Yes – he was in some old building – some kind of show-place. He had better get out quickly! He woke up Miranda, who was fast asleep in the rug, her tiny face hidden in her paws. She opened her eyes, and made a little chattering noise.

She ran up Barney's chest, as he sat up on the bed, and sat cuddled into his shoulder, pulling at one of his ears, and putting her monkey face against his cheek. He fondled her lovingly.

'You're the best little companion in the world!' he said, and tickled her. 'Aren't you, Miranda? Say – do you know who you're going to see today?'

Miranda chattered back eagerly, and Barney nodded solemnly. 'Quite right – we're visiting our friends. Now we'd better think about going. Better not shin down the ivy this time, in case someone sees us. Let's go and see if there's a back door we can open. We could slip out cautiously then.'

Barney replaced the tablecloth on the table. It looked very crumpled but he couldn't do anything about that. He put on his shoes, but stuffed his holey, rolled-up socks into his pocket. He felt his coat. It was quite dry, so he pulled that on too. There was a mirror on the wall, and he looked into it.

'Just look at that scarecrow in there, Miranda!' he said to the listening monkey. 'You might not guess it, but it's me! I wonder if there's anywhere I can wash here – or didn't these old places run to a bathroom? I guess not.'

He took a comb from his pocket and combed back his bright hair. Then he straightened the covers of the big four-poster bed, and went into the gallery that ran outside the room, overlooking the enormous room below.

He walked quietly, but there was no one about. Miranda leapt about from table to chair, from chair to chest, chattering and excited. Any strange place always pleased her.

Barney was not very interested in the old building. It meant very little to him, for he didn't know much of history. He thought some of the big wooden chairs looked extremely uncomfortable, and marvelled at the suits of armour that stood here and there round the wall. He stood and looked at one.

'Pretty small, isn't it, Miranda?' he said to the monkey. 'I could just about get into it, but only just. I reckon the old-time men couldn't have been as big as we are – tiddley little things they must have been. And fancy walking about in that, clanking all the time!'

He came to the back door, which was a massive affair, though not as enormous as the front door. He looked round for Miranda. 'Come on,' he said. 'We'll slip out here.'

There was no chattering in reply, and Miranda didn't come flying on to his shoulder. Barney looked round the room he was in. It was a huge kitchen, furnished just as it might have been two or three hundred years back. Where on earth was Miranda?

Miranda was off on a little exploration of her own. She

hadn't realised that Barney was looking for a way out. She thought he was exploring too. She had completely disappeared.

'Miranda!' called Barney softly. 'Blow you, Miranda! Where have you got to?'

He heard a little noise somewhere and went quickly in its direction. He came to the foot of the big square tower, though at first he had no idea what it was.

All he could see was the little spiral staircase going up. Up to where? Perhaps another bedroom, Barney thought. He stood and listened. Surely that tiresome little monkey hadn't gone up the stairway? A noise from above made him certain that she had.

And then another noise made him jump. Somebody was unlocking a door! 'It's the big front door!' thought Barney, scared. 'Somebody's coming in. I shall be caught.'

He glanced round. There seemed no sensible place to hide – and anyway he must get hold of Miranda and keep her quiet, or she would certainly give the game away.

He began to climb the little spiral staircase quickly, his rubber shoes making no sound on the stone. Up and up he went, and at last came to the little platform at the top. He gazed up and saw the silent bells hanging far above his head.

And up there, looking down at him cheekily, was Miranda! She was playing hide and seek with him! He had taught her that – but now she had chosen a most unfortunate time to play it!

'Miranda!' he said, in a whisper. 'Come on down! Quick!'

Miranda immediately disappeared. Barney craned his neck. Where could she be? And how had she got up so high. It was too far for her to leap.

He was in the tower. Barney could hardly see anything

except the bells high up, gleaming and silent. He felt up the wall with his hand and at last came to something he had guessed must be there.

There was a row of footholds in the stone wall of the tower on the south side. The stone was hollowed out at set places, so that a foot or hand could be inserted for climbing up. Barney slipped his hand into one hold and found that it was hollowed in such a way that his fingers could grip quite well.

He gave a little groan. Now he would have to climb all the way up in this half-darkness to get Miranda! Once she was playing hide and seek she wouldn't come to him unless he found her and cornered her. He stood on tiptoe and felt for the handholds above his head. He slipped his hands in, and then put his toes into the ones below.

He felt for the next holds and put his hands there, clutching hard with his strong fingers. It was not a very pleasant way of climbing up the steep walls of a stone tower – but Barney was used to acrobatic feats of all kinds, and he didn't really find it difficult.

As for Miranda, she must have discovered the footholds at once and climbed up easily, with glee. Barney went steadily up, slipping first his hand into the stone hollows, and then his feet. At last he was up to the bells. Now – where was Miranda?

He couldn't see her anywhere, nor hear her either. He looked cautiously round in the dim light. The bells, looking remarkably big and bright now that he was so near them, hung near his head, held by their ropes. He strained his eyes to see beyond them.

He caught sight of a pair of gleaming green eyes looking down at him. Miranda! 'You little scamp!' muttered Barney, exasperated. 'How did you get beyond the bells?'

He felt about for another handhold and found it. Then his hand found the end of a thick rope. He felt it cautiously. It didn't seem to be loose. It seemed to be fastened tightly. Was it to help a climber to go up above the bells?

Barney pulled at the rope, and it felt very firm and safe. He swarmed up it, through what looked like a hole in the roof of the tower – and found himself in a most curious place!

It was a small square room above the bells. It would have been completely dark if it hadn't been for a slit-like window set in the south side, that let in a bright ray of sunlight. Now Barney understood why the bells had gleamed so brightly when he was standing below them. This beam of sun had penetrated into the room, and a little piece of it had pierced through the hole of the floor, and fallen on the upper surface of the bells.

'So that's why they shone so curiously!' thought Barney, looking round the little stone room. There was a low bench there, very small, and a heap of what looked like rags. There was an old wooden candlestick with the remains of wax still in the bottom.

'This must have been a hidey-hole long ago,' thought Barney, kicking the rags which looked as if they had once been a rug or blanket of some kind. Miranda at once ran over to them and cuddled herself up, peeping out comically.

'I'm not too pleased with you, Miranda,' said Barney severely. 'Making me climb up all that way to get you. And now we've got to climb down again – but this time you'll be on my shoulder, and keep there – see?'

He looked out through the slit-like window. The whole countryside lay before him, smiling in the bright May sunshine. Not a cloud was in the blue sky. It made Barney long to be out there.

He suddenly felt very hungry indeed. 'Come on,

Miranda,' he said. 'We'll go and find Snubby and the others, and get some breakfast.'

Miranda knew the words breakfast, dinner, tea and supper very well indeed. She leapt on to Barney's shoulder and held on to his collar.

He let himself down through the hole in the floor, found the guide-rope, and then felt for the first footholds in the stone wall of the tower. It was easy to climb down, and soon he was standing far below the gleaming bells, on the little platform at the top of the spiral staircase.

He listened. He could hear what sounded like someone beating a mat. Perhaps the caretaker of the building was at her morning work. He might be able to slip out past her.

He went down the stone stairway very silently and carefully. He peered out at the bottom. No one was to be seen. He made his way to the front door. He caught sight of a woman in one of the rooms, dusting the old furniture. She had her back to him, so Barney took his chance and fled to the open front door. He was out in the sunshine in a trice, rejoicing to feel the warmth on his head and shoulders.

He saw the name of the old building on the gate, Ring O' Bells Hall. 'So that's where I slept for the night,' he thought. 'Ring O' Bells Hall, in Ring O' Bells Village. Very nice too!'

He debated how to find his three friends – but his difficulty didn't last long. Up the road came Roger, Diana, Snubby and the two dogs!

Barney yelled loudly. 'Ahoy there! Here we are!'

Chapter Fourteen

A Happy Meeting

Shouts, squeals, laughter, barks, chattering, back-slap-
ping – what an excitement and scurry there was, as all
the friends rushed together once more!

'Barney! Dear old Barney! We did hope you'd come
today!'

'Miranda! You're just as sweet as ever! Oh, she's leapt
on to my shoulder!'

'It's grand to see you all – Diana, you've grown. Snubby
hasn't. Hallo, Roger – it's good to see you.'

'Woof, woof, woof!'

'Barney, you're a bit taller – and as brown as ever! Oh,
do listen to Miranda chattering! I know exactly what she's
saying!'

'When did you come? How did you get here?'

'Where did you spend the night? Oh, I say – the dogs
have both gone mad.'

'Woof, woof, WOOF!'

It certainly seemed as if both the dogs had gone completely off their heads. Loony recognised Barney and
Miranda at once, of course, but Loopy didn't know them,
as he had never seen them before. But when he saw what
a tremendous welcome the excited Loony gave them,
Loopy felt he must certainly join in.

He almost outdid Loony in his excitement. He leapt up
and barked and licked and wagged and rolled over, and
altogether behaved like two Loonies rolled into one.
Loony himself got rather annoyed with him at last. These

were *his* friends, not Loopy's. What did Loopy mean by behaving like this?

Loony gave the surprised Loopy a sharp nip as if to say, 'Keep off! This is *my* welcome, not yours!'

Miranda leapt from one shoulder to another, delighted and so excited that she hardly knew what she was doing. She suddenly dropped down on Loony's back, and rode him as she always used to do. Loopy seeing this, got the surprise of his life. He backed away at once.

Miranda sprang from Loony's back on to Loopy's, and the golden spaniel ran for his life, with the cheeky little monkey jigging up and down on his back. He whined in panic.

'Woof, woof, woof! Roll over, woof!' barked Loony, running after him. So Loopy rolled over on his back, which, of course, was a sure way of dislodging Miranda. Before either dog could pounce on her she was up on Barney's shoulder again, chattering for all she was worth.

The children's excitement died down at last. They linked arms with Barney and strolled back to Miss Pepper's, quite forgetting that Miss Hannah had said she would not welcome any monkey to her house. Barney mentioned that he hadn't yet had any breakfast, and was hungry.

'Could we stop and buy some food somewhere?' he asked. 'And I'd like to buy some socks. Mine have got holes in them. I don't want to appear with holey socks.'

'You *have* got particular!' said Diana. 'You never used to mind things like that.'

'No,' said Barney, and didn't like to say that he was so proud of his friends that he wanted to be like them, and look decent if he could.

'Better come to Miss Hannah's and we'll ask her for something for you,' said Roger. 'Look at those dogs and Miranda! What a time she'll have with them!'

Miranda was sitting on a wall, holding a long twig, and was poking this at the dogs every time they tried to leap up at her. Loopy by now had decided that she was a very peculiar kind of cat, and he meant to have some fun with her.

Miss Pepper was in the front garden, picking flowers. She was delighted to see Barney. 'Just the same startlingly blue eyes and brown face!' she thought to herself, as she went to meet him. 'What a striking boy he is!'

'Miss Pepper,' said Roger when the greetings were over, 'Barney hasn't had breakfast. Can we get him some?'

'Of course!' cried Miss Pepper, and took them all inside. Miranda came too. Miss Hannah came out of the kitchen, when she heard all the excited voices – and stopped dead when she saw Miranda on Barney's shoulder. She gave a piercing scream and ran back to the kitchen, slamming the door behind her. Barney felt astonished. The others, of course, guessed at once what the matter was.

'Oh – of course – she hates monkeys!' said Roger. 'Blow – we all forgot. Miss Hannah – it's all right. I'll take Barney back to the garden, and the monkey too.'

So poor Barney was ushered back to the garden and given a deck-chair to sit in, whilst the rest went back to pacify Miss Hannah and get a meal of some kind for Barney.

Loony and Loopy remained with Barney. Loony had already given him about five hundred licks, but he still had plenty to spare, and Barney had to wipe his face with his handkerchief every minute or so.

Then Loopy began to show off to Miranda. He rushed indoors, got a mat from the hall and dragged it out at top speed, falling over whenever his hind legs got caught on

90

it. He placed it in front of Miranda, who promptly dropped down on it and sat there.

Loony watched jealously. He also disappeared into the house, and when he came back he held a large bath-towel between his teeth. He deposited it on the rug. Miranda at once took it and draped herself round in it with a very naughty air indeed.

'Woof,' said Loony to Loopy and disappeared again. He brought back somebody's hairbrush, and Miranda brushed her fur vigorously with it. Barney roared with laughter. Off went Loopy for another mat.

When Roger and the others appeared with food for Barney, the grass looked most peculiar, strewn with mats and rugs and towels, a hairbrush and a broom, which Loony with much trouble had managed to drag out by the head.

'Good gracious,' said Miss Pepper. 'Just look what those dogs have done! Are they showing off to that little Miranda?'

Diana collected everything and took mats, brushes and towels back into the house, laughing. Those two dogs! Nothing was safe from them when they took it into their heads to be silly.

The three children exchanged all their news with Barney. Barney told them of the jobs he had had since he had last seen them. They sounded remarkable to the children, even though they were used to their circus friend's doings.

'I told you I managed a troupe of monkeys – with Miranda's help,' said Barney, munching away at bread and ham. 'My word, she *did* boss those monkeys! Before that I had charge of an elephant. He was grand, that elephant.'

'What was his name?' asked Diana.

'Mr Little,' said Barney with a grin. 'He was enormous,

but very gentle and deft. You wouldn't believe it, but if you put cups and saucers down in rows in front of him, he'd walk among them without even touching a cup!'

'What else did you do?' asked Snubby.

'I took a job with a man who owned two roundabouts,' said Barney. 'That was a messy job, though. I had to oil them and see to the works. I didn't do that long. The man was mean and bad-tempered. I went to a good little job after that.'

'What was it?' said Roger.

'It was in a little theatre,' said Barney. 'Not much more than a shed, really. Different travelling companies hired it for their shows. It was my job to manage the lights and the scenery.'

'I know why you took that job,' said Diana suddenly. 'It was in case your father might come there and act!'

Barney nodded. He was always on the look-out for anyone who might be his father. He felt sure he would know him, though how, he didn't know. He didn't feel so bad about not having a father or mother now, though, because he had three good friends, and had even shared a little of their home-life at times. A home and people meant a great deal to Barney, who had none. Still, he had Miranda – she was all the world to him!

The children told him their news too – how they had had the 'flu, and had been sent away for a change and they told him about the mysterious Ring O' Bells Hall, and the secret passage and legend of the bells.

'My word! Those must be the very bells I climbed past when I went to hunt for Miranda in the tower!' said Barney, and told them about the little room above the bells. Then he remembered the strange episode of the night before, when he had seen once again the man who had given him a lift, and had heard him talking to someone in Ring O' Bells Hall.

'What was he up to, do you think, at that time of night?' asked Barney, eating the very last bit of cheese, and feeling pleasantly full. He drank his glass of milk, and got out his hanky to wipe his mouth. Before he had made friends with the children he had always wiped his mouth with the back of his hand!

'Goodness knows what anyone would be up to in this old village!' said Roger, puzzled. 'And Ring O' Bells Hall is always shut up and locked at night. Nobody is there!'

'Well, someone was definitely there late last night,' said Barney. 'And, as I say, I know who one person was, because it so happens he was the man who gave me the lift! I said I wanted to go to Lillinghame, never dreaming anyone would be going to Ring O' Bells itself. But apparently he was. He must have gone in his car, and I followed painfully on foot, not knowing he was away in front of me!'

'It's strange,' said Diana. 'And you say you heard a woman cough too – well, I should think that must have been the bad-tempered woman who guides people round the old place, and gives lectures on it. The one who showed us the secret passage but wouldn't let us go down it.'

'Perhaps she's got something down there she doesn't want anyone to see,' said Barney idly. 'After all, she's the caretaker, she can forbid people to snoop down there – what's to prevent her from hiding away anything she likes!'

'Do you mean that, Barney?' asked Diana, after a pause. It suddenly seemed to fit in with their idea of the woman, and with her behaviour.

'No – not really,' said Barney, giving Miranda a piece of an orange. 'I just said it. Why? You seem to have gone all serious about it.'

'You know – I think we ought to examine that secret

passage,' said Roger. 'Just to make sure there *isn't* something peculiar going on down there!'

Chapter Fifteen

A Wonderful Day

Miss Pepper came out and interrupted this most interesting conversation. 'Barney, have you had enough?' she asked. 'Sure? Well, listen. My cousin Miss Hannah really *is* scared of monkeys, she's so scared she's quite likely to faint if Miranda comes near her. It's a pity, but there it is. So I thought as it's such fine weather you could all go off for the day together, and take your meals with you.'

'Wizard!' said Snubby and Roger at once, and Diana's face shone. Barney got up politely and smiled.

'Nothing I should like better,' he said. 'And I quite understand about your cousin, Miss Pepper. I won't come further than the front gate in future.'

'It's very nice of you not to mind, Barney,' said Miss Pepper. 'Hannah is very sorry about it – and she's packing up a most exciting lunch and tea for you to take with you, just to make up to you for her unfortunate dislike of monkeys.'

'Goody!' said Diana, pleased. 'Where shall we go? I know! Let's go through Ring O' Bells Wood, and walk through the bridle path all the way to the top of the hill where we rode to yesterday. It would be heavenly.'

'Woof,' said Loony approvingly. He had heard the word 'walk', which always seemed to him to be one of the most sensible words in the language of humans. 'Bone' was another and 'Dinner' was the third. A conversation made up of these three words, with perhaps 'Biscuit' and 'Chocolate' and 'Rats' and 'Rabbits' thrown in occasionally would have interested Loony very much.

'Let't go and see old Red Riding Hood in Ring O' Bells Cottage on our way,' suggested Snubby. Barney looked surprised.

'Who's she? I've never heard of an *old* Red Riding Hood before,' he said. 'All the ones I've seen in panto-mimes have been young.'

'Well, wait till you see ours,' grinned Snubby. 'And wait till you see her green eyes! We think she's the grand-daughter of a witch.'

'Don't be idiotic, Snubby,' said Roger. 'Di, hadn't you better go and see if Miss Hannah wants a bit of help with the sandwich-packing? There's a lot to cut up and pack, I should think!'

Diana went. Miss Hannah was pleased to see her, and let her arrange slices of tongue on the bread cut for sandwiches. There seemed quite a mound of cut slices! 'Have I cut enough?' asked Miss Hannah anxiously. 'My cousin said you all ate twice as much out of doors as in, and that scared me a bit. I don't want you to go hungry.'

'We shan't,' said Diana, eyeing the loaded table. Sand-wiches, sausage rolls, hard-boiled eggs, bread and butter to go with them, tomatoes, lettuce, slices of thick, solid fruit cake, biscuits in a packet, bars of chocolate – good gracious, what a picnic it would be!

She gave Miss Hannah a sudden hug. 'You're awfully nice,' she said. 'As nice as Miss Pepper. Thank you very much.'

Miss Hannah went red with pleasure, and put an extra lot of butter on the bit of bread she was buttering. She liked these children, noisy though they were, and quite mad at times. But they had nice ways and good manners and were always ready to help. You just couldn't help liking them, even that monkey of a Snubby. That reminded Miss Hannah of Miranda and she gave a shudder.

'Do see that the monkey doesn't come anywhere near me, won't you, Diana?' she said beseechingly. 'Why, the very thought makes my legs turn to water!'

Diana glanced with interest at Miss Hannah's legs, but they seemed just the same as usual – not even wobbly as Snubby's had been. She finished putting the tongue in the very last sandwich.

There was so much food and drink that Miss Hannah had to find three satchels to put it in, for the boys to carry. Snubby didn't see why Diana shouldn't take her share of the carrying and said so.

'I'm *going* to take my share of the load, Snubby,' said Diana. 'But you might at least let Miss Hannah go on thinking you're a perfect little gentleman – though how anyone can think that, I really – '

She had to stop and laugh, because Snubby picked up a cushion to smother her. Anyway, who could quarrel or bicker on such a day, when they had got Barney and Miranda back with them, and a whole day's picnicking in front of them!

'I hope you won't be lonely, Miss Pepper,' called Snubby kindly as they set off down the front path.

'Oh, it'll be quite a *nice* loneliness!' called back Miss Hannah. 'Don't you worry about us. We shall get on quite well without you.'

Miranda was on Barney's shoulder as usual. The two dogs, their tails wagging furiously, capered round and round, getting in everyone's way. They knew by the satchels on the boys' backs that this was to be a long, long walk!

It certainly was a wonderful day. The four children and the animals went up through Ring O' Bells Wood, and when they came to the little path that led off to Ring O' Bells Cottage, they debated whether or not to go and have a look at it, or to call on their way back.

'On our way back,' decided Roger. 'Old Red Riding Hood might give us a glass of milk or something then. We shall probably be thirsty on our way home.'

'All right,' said Diana. 'Come on – up the broad path we go. Loony, that's not a rabbit-hole – that's where a tree had been uprooted.'

They walked through the wood, which was dim and cool on this hot May day. Bluebells were coming out everywhere, and lay like pools of shimmering amethyst among the trees. The children sniffed the sweet smell, with just as much enjoyment as the two dogs sniffed rabbit-smells.

'Look at those wind-flowers – there are hundreds of them!' said Diana. Barney stood with her and watched the pretty, star-like flowers dancing in the wind. Barney didn't know many flower-names, and he liked to learn them. Diana knew such a lot! She enjoyed teaching Barney. He was a very willing pupil, with an excellent memory.

They had their lunch on the very top of the hill, overlooking the valley. Far away in the distance they could see the gleam of the Bristol Channel, thrusting up from the sea. It was dazzling silver in the sun, though it would turn blue later in the day.

'This is a most magnificent lunch,' said Barney, biting into a hard-boiled egg. 'Where's the salt? Anyone remember it?'

'I did,' said Diana, and gave him the screw of paper with the salt inside. 'Look out – don't let the wind blow it all away.'

The four children worked their way through most of the food. They left very little for tea. 'We really ought to stop eating,' said Diana, examining what was left. 'We're sure to be hungry for tea, and we've eaten nearly everything.'

'Perhaps old Red Riding Hood will offer us tea,' suggested Snubby.

'Why should she?' said Diana. 'I should think she'd be scared of four like us. We've got frightful appetites. Everyone says so.'

'Snubby only said that because he'd like to finish everything now,' said Roger, and gave Snubby a poke in his fat middle.

'*Don't*!' said Snubby, in alarm. 'I've eaten too much to be jabbed in the middle.'

This was the kind of silly, friendly talk that Barney enjoyed, and got nowhere else in his life. Most of the circus children he knew were rough and cheeky, and the adults he had lived with had no use for simple friendly talk like this. Barney listened to every word and enjoyed it. How nice to be a family and know each other so well! He thought he was very lucky to be friendly with this one.

The dogs had their share of the food, and Miranda ate a banana daintily, peeling it herself. She threw the skin on the grass. 'Now then, Miranda, manners!' said Barney sternly. 'Pick that up at once. We don't leave litter about.'

Miranda picked up the banana skin and hopped on to Roger's shoulder. She suddenly stuffed it down his neck, and leapt away chattering with glee at his yell of dismay. He put it into the bag of bits and pieces that was to go into one of the satchels and be taken home to be burnt.

It was a long lazy day, and by the time three o'clock came they were red-brown with the hot sun, all except Barney, who was already so brown that he couldn't possibly get any browner!

'It's time we went back,' said Roger lazily. 'Where are those dogs? It's a good thing rabbit-holes aren't any bigger, or both of them would be wandering lost for ever in a maze of warrens!'

'They never learn they can't get down,' said Diana. 'If

I were a rabbit I'd sit a little way down the hole, where I could see Loony's black face poking down at me, and laugh my head off at him.'

'That's just what rabbits probably do,' said Snubby. 'I've often wondered what it is that makes Loony go so dippy about digging out rabbit-holes – he's probably feeling furious with a grinning rabbit sitting a little way down.'

The dogs came back at last, their noses sandy, and their tongues hanging almost to the ground! They flopped down beside the children.

'Up you get,' said Roger, getting up himself. 'We're starting back on the way home. We're making a call on the way, Loony, on Red Riding Hood. Look out for the wolf!'

They walked leisurely down the long slope of the hill, and reached the wood. The bluebells were a deeper blue now, and the wind-flowers no longer danced because there was no breeze. It was very hot indeed.

'I could do with a drink of water,' said Roger. 'If I had a tongue long enough it would be hanging out on my chest!'

'Here's the little path that leads to Red Riding Hood's Cottage,' said Diana at last, and they turned down it and walked till they came in sight of the little house.

'Honestly, it's a fairy-tale house!' said Diana, as they came near. She was right. It was. It looked as crooked and tumble-down as a cottage in a tale, its chimneys were surprisingly tall, its windows small and diamond-paned. Bluebells grew right up to the little wall that surrounded it.

'There's an old well in the garden,' said Diana, pointing. 'I say – isn't it an adorable place. I do hope old Red Riding Hood is in!'

Chapter Sixteen

Ring O' Bells Cottage

They opened the little white gate and walked up a tiny flagged path to the front door. It was painted blue, as were the shutters outside the windows. Diana knocked.

'Come in!' said a voice, and Diana opened the door. Inside was a small room, perfectly square, with a big fireplace at one end. The uneven floor was of stone. Old Riding Hood was standing over the fire, stirring something in a pot.

But she wasn't wearing her old red cloak and hood, so she didn't look like Red Riding Hood any more. The cloak hung on a nail nearby.

Naomi Barlow looked out of her green-grey eyes at the children. They were disappointed to see that her eyes didn't seem nearly so green as they had imagined. Still, she looked a bit of a fairy-tale person still, with her white apron, red shawl, and snow-white hair.

'Well! If it isn't Miss Hannah's visitors!' she said. 'Sit you down, and I'll get you some home-made biscuits. I'm sorry I've no milk to offer you, for you must be rarely thirsty this hot day. Would you like some ice-cold water out of my well?'

This sounded good. 'Yes, please,' said Roger at once. 'Can I go and get some? Is there a bucket on a chain, and a handle that winds?'

'Yes,' said Naomi. Then she suddenly caught sight of Miranda on Barney's shoulder. 'Why, the little mite!' she said, and left her pot and came over to Barney. 'I once had a monkey of my own. It was left for dead by a circus that once came to Ring O' Bells. I took it and nursed it and it lived with me many a year.'

She fussed over Miranda, which made Loony and Loopy jealous. She seemed quite at home with children, dogs and monkey. They all liked her.

Roger went out with Barney to get the water. They took a large white jug that Naomi had given them.

'What an enormous well for such a small place,' said Roger, in surprise. 'I bet it's deep.'

It was. It was so very deep that neither of the boys could see the water. Roger took a stone and dropped it down. It was quite a time before he heard the splash. He peered down.

'It's a nice well,' he said. 'It's got ferns and things growing all the way down the sides. I bet the water's cold!'

He and Barney wound the bucket down till it reached the water. Then they wound it up again, the chain making quite a noise. They took the bucket off and emptied the water into the big jug. 'Feel it,' said Barney. 'Absolutely icy-cold!'

They all enjoyed drinking the crystal-clear cold water, and eating Naomi's home-made biscuits. They tasted of cinnamon, and were very spicy indeed. She put some into a bag for them.

The children asked to see round the cottage. 'There's not much to see,' said old Naomi. 'Just three tiny rooms! This is my parlour-kitchen, where I cook and sit. And this is my bedroom.'

The bedroom was even smaller than the kitchen. The children looked at the flat stone floor, and thought how cold it must be in the winter. The kitchen was the same, set with big, solid, white flags, a little uneven here and there.

'And this is my store-room,' said Naomi, opening a

door off the kitchen, and showing them a cupboard of a room. She had made it into a store-room, and there were jars of pickles, jam, honey spices, and all kinds of things. It too had a cold stone floor, and even on that hot May day, it seemed chilly to the children.

'That was my bedroom when I was a girl,' said Naomi. 'I slept there for years. Then when my old Dad died and Ma followed him, I made it into a store-room. Barlows have lived here for years upon years – four hundred years, so I've heard tell. But there won't be a Barlow here after me, more's the pity.'

It was a quaint, peculiar, uncomfortable old cottage, too dark with its too-small, leaded windows, and probably far too cold, with its solid stone floor, in the winter. But, as Diana said afterwards, 'it had a lovely *feeling* about it, it was full of old thoughts and old doings, and past and gone days.'

'Mother Barlow must have lived there too,' said Snubby, as they went home. 'I'd like to have known her. I do wonder why Old Grandad kept saying, 'Ask Mother Barlow, ask Mother Barlow,' the other day, when we wanted to know where the secret passage went. Why should *she* know so much about it?'

'Because she probably used it, and caught him!' said Roger. 'I say – what about Barney's lodgings tonight? I was thinking he'd be coming home with us, but of course he can't. We'd better ask in the village if there's anywhere for him to sleep!'

So they asked, first at the village stores, and then at the various addresses that the woman there gave them.

But although many would have been willing to take Barney, nobody wanted Miranda. In vain Barney and the others sang her praises, said she was quite harmless, and very sweet and good-mannered – nobody would have Miranda!

'She'd bring fleas,' said one.

'She'd bite my baby,' said another.

'I don't hold with monkeys,' said a third.

And so it went on – no, no, no, till the children got quite desperate.

Barney, of course, didn't mind. He was used to sleeping anywhere, in a caravan, in a tent, under a hedge or a haystack.

'Don't you bother about me,' he kept saying, but the children did. Diana pointed out that great clouds had rolled up again and threatened the same downpour of rain as the night before.

'You simply *must* be under cover,' she said

'All right,' said Barney. 'What's the matter with me sleeping in the Ring O' Bells Hall again? Nobody sleeps there, and I shan't do any harm.'

'Well, you could,' said Roger. 'I can't see what it would really matter. What's the time? I believe it would still be open. Let's go and see. If it is, we'll pay and go in, and find a better place for you to sleep than the four-poster bed you spoke about. We can leave you there!

The woman looked sourly at them when they arrived in the hall, having tied up the two dogs securely. 'It's just upon closing time,' she said.

'There's five minutes to go,' said Roger firmly, and he placed the money on the table, 'We want to show our friend around.'

The woman caught sight of the monkey. 'Not with that monkey!' she said. But the children had already marched on down the hall.

'Show me the room where that secret passage is,' said Barney suddenly. 'I'd like to see that.'

'Right,' said Roger. 'But we can't look at the passage because you have to pay extra for that, and I don't want to go back to that bad-tempered woman! Now let's see – which room was it?'

They went into two or three and then found the little room into which the secret passage opened. Roger showed Barney the big tapestry picture which could be moved to one side in order to open the tiny panel that had to be used to move the lever that freed the big panel.

'Sounds like the House-that-Jack-built to me!' said Barney, with a grin. 'Move the picture to open the panel to move the lever to free the panel, to–'

'It does sound a bit complicated,' said Roger, 'I tell you what – we'll come one day and explore that passage all by ourselves. Though how we're going to do it without that woman suspecting, I don't know.'

'Have to come one night then,' said Barney. Diana shivered.

'I only hope the bells don't ring then!' she said.

'They wouldn't. We're not enemies!' said Snubby. 'I say – that would be a bit of an adventure, wouldn't it – to explore a secret passage one night!'

'I think I'll sleep in the little room here for the night,' said Barney, looking round. 'There's a big couch with cushions – though they look pretty hard – and I could take that cloth off the table over there to put round me. You wouldn't believe how warm the table-cloth was last night! I shall be very comfortable here.'

A voice came sharply from the hall. 'I'm just closing the place. Will you please come, or you'll be locked in!'

'She doesn't guess that one of us *wants* to be locked in!' whispered Snubby in glee. 'So long, Barney. Sleep well. See you in the morning.'

'Take old Red Riding Hood's biscuits for your supper,' said Diana, pushing the paper bag into Barney's hand. 'And here's the rest of the chocolate. Come up to Miss

Hannah's in the morning and wait outside the gate. We'll bring you breakfast.'

'Thanks,' said Barney, gratefully. The others went quickly out of the room and looked round the hall. The woman could be heard locking up somewhere at the back. Now was their time to go, before she realised that only three were departing instead of four!

'Good night!' called Roger, in a stentorian voice and Snubby and Diana joined in. There might have been a dozen of them, not three!

The woman made no answer. The children went out quickly, grinning at one another. It was easy! They untied the impatient dogs and went off up the road to Miss Hannah's rambling old house.

'Barney will be all right in that little room,' said Roger, glancing up at the overcast sky. 'Here comes the first big drops. Hurry!'

They hurried, glad to think that Barney and Miranda wouldn't have to sleep under a hedge. They ran in at the gate, and were welcomed by Miss Pepper.

'*Just* in time!' she said. 'I was afraid you'd be caught by the storm. Did you have a good day?'

'Wonderful!' said Diana. 'Where's Miss Hannah? We want to tell her that the food was absolutely super!'

'Wizard,' said the boys, together. 'We ate it all!'

'What have you done with Barney and Miranda?' asked Miss Pepper, as they went indoors. 'I hope you found him lodgings of some kind.'

Roger grinned. 'Yes – we did. He'll be quite comfortable, Miss Pepper. He's got a *very* nice little room of his own, with nobody to disturb him at all!'

Chapter Seventeen

In The Middle Of The Night

Barney certainly had a nice little room of his own! He felt quite glad to be there, too, when he heard the thunder crashing and the rain pelting down. The caretaker-woman had gone, slamming the front door behind her. He was quite alone, except for Miranda.

Barney waited for the slamming of the front door, and then he stood up. He didn't want to go to bed yet! He wondered if there were any books about that he might read.

He had crouched by a chest waiting for the caretaker to go, ready to open the lid and slip inside, if she came near. But she didn't. She apparently thought that all the children had gone, and that the place was quite empty.

'And now I'm master of Ring O' Bell Hall,' said Barney, out loud, as he wandered through the great mansion. He went into the kitchen and marvelled at the enormous cooking stoves there. What meals they must have cooked in the old days here! He went idly to the tap over the great wide sink and turned it on, not expecting any water to come out.

But a stream of cold water splashed at once into the sink. Barney found an old tankard on a shelf and filled it. He drank deeply, for the night was hot and he was really very thirsty. He rinsed out the tankard and put it back. He supposed that water was laid on for the caretaker to use. Well, that was lucky for *him*!

He found some books in a panelled room that looked like a library. In fact, he found about two thousand books.

They lined the shelves from floor to ceiling, most of them leather-bound. Their colours were old and faded now, and looked as if nobody had ever read them.

Barney took one or two down. They were printed in old-time lettering and he found them too difficult to understand. He put them back carefully, noting that they were very dusty. The caretaker-woman needed to take her duster round a bit more, he though!

It was dull all by himself, and he was glad when he felt sleepy. He ate all the biscuits and the chocolate that Diana had given him, and then got another drink of water. He gave Miranda a drink too, and a few raisins to eat.

'And don't you put the pips down my neck this time, and don't you spit them out, either!' he said. 'Put them into your paw and give them to me.'

So for once in a way Miranda was very polite, and spat each pip into her tiny brown paw, and handed them solemnly to Barney, who just as solemnly put them into an ashtray on one of the tables.

When it was almost dark, he took the tablecloth off the table a carried it to the big couch. He arranged the cushions for his head and then lay down. He pulled the big cloth over him. It was heavy and warm – too warm after a while, and Barney had to push it partly off him.

Miranda cuddled into his jacket, putting her little paws inside his shirt. He liked to feel them there. He blew softly on the top of her head.

'Good night, Miranda. Sleep well, and we won't wake up before morning!'

But he was wrong – they did!

Miranda woke first, and lay cuddled against Barney, her ears twitching. What had awakened her? She lay listening, and then settled down again. But before she had fallen asleep once more, her ears twitched again. This time she scrambled out of Barney's coat and sat on the head of the couch. She chattered a little in a very small voice indeed.

She awoke Barney, and he sat up, feeling for Miranda. Where had she gone? He heard her low chattering nearby and put out a hand to touch her. She nestled into his arms at once.

'What woke you, Miranda?' Barney whispered. 'Something disturbed you. What was it. It's the middle of the night. Did you hear a mouse or a rat?'

On the night air came the sound of the church clock striking some distance away. Doing – dong – dong.

'Three o'clock,' said Barney. 'There's still a lot of the night left, Miranda. Go to sleep.'

And then he too heard a noise. At first he thought he must be mistaken. Then it came again. Where was it? Surely it wasn't in the room? It was a curious noise, and it came and went in spasms. What did it sound like?

Barney decided that the noise certainly wasn't in the room. He felt in his pocket for the torch that Roger had lent him. He switched it on. The beam flashed round the room. It was quite empty. There was nobody and nothing there.

The noise could not be heard outside the little room where he had been sleeping. He soon made certain of that. He then went carefully round the room, stopping and listening at various points.

He came to one place where the noise sounded loudest. He flashed his torch on the spot. It was the panel which Roger had pointed out to him as the one that opened into the secret passage. He pressed his ear to it.

Now he could hear the noise much better, when it came. It was a curious, spasmodic noise, fairly regular, but too far away to make out whether it was made by a machine, or by a human being or animal, or by water – in fact Barney couldn't make it out at all. It came spasmodically, but it was always the same when it did come – a series of quick sounds more or less regularly spaced. Barney guessed they came up from the secret passage, and were altered considerably before they reached him because of the distance and the hollowness of the secret passage.

He didn't know how to open the secret passage, so he couldn't find out anything. He went back to lie down on the couch, with Miranda beside him.

'Might as well go to sleep,' he told the little monkey. 'We're not likely to find out anything by just listening to those sounds for hours. But – I think we certainly ought to examine that secret passage, Miranda. What do you suppose is down there?'

Miranda hadn't the faintest idea. She cuddled down again and went to sleep. So did Barney. Whether the noises went on again or not, he didn't know and he didn't care.

Barney awoke in good time in the morning and got up cautiously, in case the caretaker had come early. But the whole building was silent. There was not even the mysterious sound he had heard in the middle of the night.

He wondered if he could have dreamt it. No, he couldn't, he remembered it too well. He stole into the kitchen to put his face under the tap and to get a drink.

Miranda pretended to hold her paws out to the tap, but she didn't get wet. She wasn't fond of water!

'You're a fraud,' said Barney, drying himself on his big red handkerchief. 'No, I'm not going to dry your paws when they're not even wet. You wash your hands properly then I will.'

He went back to the little room where he had slept and made it tidy, draping the tablecloth over the table again. He wondered if the caretaker would notice how crumpled it was, and be puzzled. He didn't think she noticed much

110

though, judging by the layers of dust she had left here and there.

He went into the hall to watch for her coming. He didn't like to go out of the back door, leaving it unlocked, in case she was suspicious.

He hid behind the big chest and waited. She should be coming soon. In a little while he heard her footsteps coming down the path outside, then she slid the big key into the door and opened it.

As soon as she had disappeared into one of the rooms Barney slipped out with Miranda. Nobody saw him. He made his way to Miss Hannah's house and stood by the front gate, waiting.

Snubby rushed out to him. 'Barney! I've been watching for you. We're in the middle of breakfast and I'll bring a tray out for you here. You can sit in the garden, Miss Hannah says, if you'll promise not to let Miranda off your shoulder.'

When the others come out after breakfast Barney told them of his peculiar experience in the middle of the night. 'I can't imagine what it was,' he said. 'It was a silly sort of noise. I can't place it, and yet I feel I know it and have heard it many times. But, of course the hollowness of the passage must make it sound very different from what it really is.'

The others listened, amazed and thrilled. 'Did it *really* come from behind the panelling, Barney?' asked Roger. 'What's down there then? That woman says the passage is walled up, so whatever is there can't be very far down!'

'It sounded a good way down,' said Barney. 'Are you all game to explore it?'

They were – though Diana sounded a bit quavery. Snubby felt very brave sitting out there in the bright sunshine, discussing weird noises that happened in the night – but he couldn't help wondering if he would feel quite so brave in the dead of night!

'That woman would never let us go down in the day-time, that's certain,' said Roger. 'So it means we must explore after she's gone home. But we can't very well slip out before supper, or Miss Pepper would want to know what we're up to with you. We'd better come after we're supposed to be in bed.'

They debated it solemnly, and decided it would be best to go then. Miss Pepper and Miss Hannah went to bed very early, about nine o'clock. The children could easily dress and slip out. Nobody would know.

'Right,' said Barney, finishing his breakfast. 'That's settled then. Tonight about half-past nine. We'll do the "This is the-House-that-Jack-Built" business – move the picture that slides the panel that works the lever that frees the panel that opens the passage that lets us go down, that brings us to – '

'What?' cried the other three eagerly. But Barney shook his head. 'That's as far as I can get,' he said. 'We'll know the rest of our little story tonight, I hope. Now if you've got to do some jobs for Miss Hannah, I'll take the two dogs for a walk. They're pawing at me as if they want to get my jacket off! All right, all right, Loony and Loopy. I'll take you for a walkie-walk and get some of your fat off!'

He went off with the two dogs, whistling his lovely clear whistle. The others went back to help with the various jobs.

'Tonight – at half-past nine!' thought Diana, with a little shiver. 'It's exciting – but I do feel a little bit scared!'

Chapter Eighteen

Down the Secret Passage

At half-past nine that night Miss Pepper and Miss Hannah were both in bed, and Miss Hannah was fast asleep. The children were ready to go and were debating whether to take Loony or not.

'Will he bark the place down if we don't take him?' whispered Diana.

'Yes,' whispered back Snubby. 'We'd better let him come. I'll carry him downstairs so that his great paws don't make a noise.'

So Loony was carried downstairs, puzzled but very good and quiet. Loony slept on a couch in Miss Hannah's room, which was fortunately in another wing of the house, so he heard nothing.

They all heaved a sigh of relief when they were safely out on the road, walking softly in the moonlight. They soon arrived at Ring O' Bells Hall, and Barney let them in at the front door. He closed it quietly.

'Have you heard those noises again?' asked Snubby. Barney shook his head.

'No. Not tonight. Not a sound. Come on, let's go to the little room and get going.'

They went to the room where Barney had slept the night before, and where the entrance of the secret passage was. All of them had torches, and they shone them on the big tapestry picture on the wall.

'See that face with a helmet pushed back on the fore-head?' said Roger in a low voice. 'Well, watch – I press it just *here* – and see what happens!'

The picture slid quietly to one side, exposing the small panel. Roger pressed on it and the panel slid aside in its turn. He put in his hand and felt for the knob. He pressed that too, and at the same moment a small rattling noise came from behind another panel some distance away on the wall.

Barney looked startled. 'That's the lever freeing the other panel, so that we can push it to one side,' whispered Diana. They went to the second panel which was large. Roger pushed against it hard, and to Barney's surprise it slid to one side, passing neatly under the panel next to it, disclosing the yawning hole that was the entrance to the secret passage.

Loony gave a tiny yelp. He couldn't understand all these curious happenings by the light of torches. 'Shut up,' said Snubby, tapping the dog's head. 'Don't say a word, Loony.'

Roger thrust his torch inside the panelling and tried to see the passage. But all he could make out was a dark and narrow way behind the panelling.

'Shall we get in and follow the passage now?' whispered Roger. 'It's all quiet – nothing to be heard at all!'

'Right – you go first, Roger, then Diana can go, then Snubby and I'll follow with Loony,' said Barney. 'It's so narrow we'll have to go in single file.'

Roger got in, lifting his leg over the panelling. He stood in the passage, which smelt dusty and musty. He moved along a little way and one by one all the others got into it too. Loony was lifted in by Snubby.

He was surprised and very subdued. He thought this was a most peculiar evening!

'Where's Miranda?' whispered Snubby.

'She wouldn't come into the hole,' whispered back Barney. 'She was scared. She'll be all right in that room. She'll wait for us.'

The passage was indeed dark and narrow. It went behind the panelling of the room for about twelve feet and then turned abruptly to the left. It then went downwards by means of very shallow steps, down and down and down.

Roger was in front, keeping his torch level so that its light flashed on what was before him. Once he stopped, and the whole line bumped into one another.

'What's up, Roger?' asked Diana anxiously.

'Look,' said Roger, and flashed his torch on two tiny wooden doors set in a hole in the wall at one side of the passage. 'A cupboard! Perhaps the very cupboard where Old Grandad found those books and the carved box!'

He opened the doors, expecting the cupboard to be empty. But it wasn't. What it held was rather surprising. Nothing old, but something very new and modern. There were torch batteries, candles, a little tin of paraffin oil, and a dozen boxes of matches.

'What strange things to store here,' said Diana, looking at them. 'I suppose they've been left here ever since the passage was walled up – maybe they were useful for exploring it before the roof fell in and they closed it.'

'That was a long time ago,' said Roger. He shut the cupboard doors thoughtfully and went on once more, picking his way slowly. The passage was much wider once it left the panelling. Roger reckoned that it was really a tunnel now, going underground. Possibly it had left the house behind and was no longer underneath it. The caretaker-woman had told them that it avoided the cellars, which, presumably, spread themselves under the house.

He suddenly stopped again, with a short exclamation. The others did their usual bumping. Loony whined.

'You might give us warning when you're going to stop so suddenly,' grumbled Snubby under his breath. 'What's up now?'

Roger was flashing his torch on what looked like a brick wall in front of him. It stretched from ground to roof. 'Here's the wall that woman told us of,' he said. 'The passage *is* bricked up then! Look at that! We can't go any farther!'

This was bitterly disappointing. None of the children had really believed in their hearts that the woman had spoken the truth. But she had. There was the wall! If there was any more of the secret passage it must be on the other side of the wall, and she had said that the roof had fallen in there.

'What a swizz!' said Snubby.

'What about the noises Barney heard? We haven't come across anything that could make them,' whispered Roger. This was passed back to Barney.

'Funny,' said Barney. 'Where could they have come from then?'

'Let's go back,' said Diana. 'I don't like the smell down here.'

So back they went, turning themselves round and having Barney for leader this time. They passed the unusual little cupboard but didn't open it again. Then they were up behind the panelling, and in a moment or two were climbing out of the passage and into the room beyond.

Roger pressed the panel back into place. A rattling noise came as it slid back. That was the lever moving back against the panel to prevent anyone opening it unless they pressed the hidden knob behind the picture. Roger then slid back the little panel, and wondered how to move back the picture into place. He couldn't find out, so it had to be left out of place.

'Perhaps that woman will think she left it out of place herself, if she notices it tomorrow,' said Diana. 'I say – what a disappointment. I don't quite know what I expected to find, but I expected *some*thing. But we didn't even hear one of Barney's noises!'

'Sh!' said Barney, suddenly. 'I believe I did hear it again – just then. Hush, everyone!'

They all stiffened, and listened hard. Yes, there *was* a noise – a few quick, regular sounds, far away and hollow-sounding. It *did* seem as if it came up the secret passage, muffled and distant.

'There you are,' said Barney. 'I began to think I'd dreamt it – but I hadn't.'

And then they suddenly heard another noise – quite a different noise, that made them go tense and clutch one another.

It was only a small sound – a tiny jangle of a noise – as if – as if one of the bells up in the tower had moved, and its clapper had bumped against it!

'That was a bell-noise,' breathed Diana. 'And it came from the tower. Oh, don't say the bells are going to ring themselves!'

And then it happened. The bells rang out, jingled and jangled, clashed and rang away up in the tower! Diana clutched Roger so tightly that her nails went into the flesh of his arm. Loony howled dismally.

The bells suddenly stopped. The echo of the clanging died away, and Diana sank down on the couch, trembling. Snubby was petrified and couldn't move. Barney and Roger spoke together softly.

'Who rang them? There's nobody here but ourselves.'

'And anyway there are no ropes to pull. Why did they suddenly ring?'

'In the old days it was said that they rang because enemies were coming. Surely the bells don't count us as enemies! They couldn't have rung against *us*!'

'Bells can't ring themselves,' said Roger, trying to convince himself that they couldn't. But they *had* rung themselves! The children had heard them.

A little scared, whimpering noise made them all jump.

'Oh – *poor* little Miranda!' said Diana, picking the tiny monkey up. 'Did the bells scare you too? Never mind. It's all right now.'

'Do you think we dare to go and look in the square tower, just to see if anyone has rigged up ropes to peal the bells?' asked Roger, after a time. They were now all sitting close together on the couch, trying to recover from their fright.

'I'm not going,' said Snubby promptly. 'They might begin to ring again and I'd have a double fit!'

'I'm going to see,' said Barney and walked off. Roger followed him rather reluctantly.

They soon came back. 'No ropes at all,' said Barney. 'The bells are all quite still. There's nothing to be seen. Well – I don't know who the enemies are – but *I* can't see or hear any. The bells made a mistake *this* time!'

'*Listen*,' said Diana urgently. 'I can hear something. I can really – out in the hall there.'

They listened tensely. They heard a key being thrust into the front door, and somebody opened it. There were voices – footsteps! The door closed softly.

'The bells were right!' whispered Snubby. 'These must be the enemies!'

Chapter Nineteen

All Very Peculiar

'We must hide!' said Barney. 'They may come in here.'
Fortunately the footsteps went into the kitchen, and the
children could hear water running. They looked round
the little room desperately. They didn't dare to leave it
in case they were seen.

A great chest stood in one corner, and a smaller one
in another. Barney lifted up the lid of the large one. 'Get
in,' he whispered to the others. 'There's room for three
of you. I'll get into the other with Miranda.'

They got in hurriedly, making as little noise as possible.
Snubby dragged poor Loony in, tapping him fiercely on
the head every time he showed an inclination to growl.
Barney slipped inside the other chest. But Miranda ref-
used to come! She shot away from him in the darkness.
She hated being shut up anywhere.

Barney gave a little groan. He hoped Miranda would
keep out of the way of the 'enemy' whoever they were.
What in the world were people doing here at this time of
night?

They had only just hidden themselves in time. Footsteps
– two pairs – came into the room where they were hidden.

'Where is he?' said a man's voice.

'I'll take you to him.' It was a woman's voice that
answered – the caretaker! Barney lifted up the lid of his
chest a fraction and listened.

He heard the now familiar rattle behind the panelling
as the lever fell back to release the larger panel. Ah –
they were going down the secret passage then. Why?

There was nothing there. It was blocked up not very far down. Barney was puzzled. The woman had apparently not noticed that the big picture was out of place, which was a relief.

He saw her by the light of the man's torch. He couldn't see the man very well, but noticed that he had a bag, a small attaché case of some kind. His voice was deep and rough. He didn't sound at all pleased.

Loony growled suddenly – a deep, blood-curdling noise from the depths of the large chest. The woman and the man stood still, as if transfixed.

'What in the name of goodness was that?' said the man at last. 'What a fearful noise!'

From above his head came a small gibbering sound. That was Miranda, of course, telling Loony to be quiet! It made the man and woman jump violently. The man swung his torch upwards, but Miranda had gone. She gibbered from the opposite side of the room now.

Loony growled again, and was immediately stifled by Snubby.

'There's that frightful noise again,' – said the man. 'It's enough to give anyone the creeps. What's the matter with this place?'

'Nothing,' said the woman, in a trembling voice. 'I've never heard these noises before. But it can't be anything – just – just owls or something.'

'Owls don't make blood-curdling noises like that,' said the man, switching his torch into the yawning hole in the panelling. 'Well, come on – do we really have to get in here?'

The woman gave a sudden scream, and Barney almost dropped the lid of the chest in surprise. Now what was happening?

Miranda had sat herself on a shelf near the woman's

head, and had pulled at her hair. No wonder she screamed.

She made the man jump, and he became angry. 'Stop it!' he growled. 'We're getting nerves or something. What's the matter now?'

'S-s-s-something pulled my hair,' the woman quavered.

'And so will I if you don't stop all this play-acting,' said the man. He gave the woman a shove and she went into the secret passage more quickly than she had intended to. He followed. Barney could hear their steps going along behind the panelling, and then down the shallow steps underground. He opened the lid wide and jumped out, padding across the floor to the opening in the panelling. He put his head in and listened.

But except for a scraping kind of noise which he couldn't make out, he heard no more. All was silence. Where had the two gone?

He ran lightly to the other chest and opened it.

'Come on,' he said. 'Now's our chance to go. They've gone down the secret passage, goodness knows where or why. We'd better clear out. I don't like this much.'

The others gladly scrambled out. They shut the lid down and ran quietly in their rubber-soled shoes to the door. They sidled into the dark hall and made for the front door, which they knew was directly opposite. Barney thought it would be safe to switch on his torch for half a second.

They came to the front door and Barney opened it quietly. He would have to leave it open because he couldn't risk making a noise when he closed it. He suddenly put out a warning hand to the others.

'Be careful. There may be a car waiting somewhere,' he said. 'We don't want to be seen.'

He looked sharply out to the road, and made out a dim red light – the rear light of a car!

'We'll go round the house to the back,' he whispered. 'We can squeeze through a hedge and into the lane farther up. Come on. Don't make a sound!'

They all breathed more freely when at last they were some way up the lane, having squeezed through the hedge halfway down the garden of Ring O' Bells Hall. Loony was completely bewildered. What kind of game was this, played so late at night? He was tired of being tapped on the head by Snubby when he wanted to growl.

'Don't say anything till we get back to Miss Pepper's,' said Roger, in a low voice. So, feeling that there might be ears listening in every hedge, the four of them hurried quietly back.

They went to a little shed in Miss Hannah's garden and crowded in there together. 'What an evening,' said Roger, blowing out a deep breath of relief at being somewhere ordinary and safe. 'Those bells ringing out all by themselves like that – and then the woman and the man coming, exactly as if they were the enemies foretold by the bells.'

'I wonder if anyone else heard them – the villagers, for instance,' said Diana.

'Some of them may have,' said Roger. 'But the village is a little way away, isn't it – and as the bells are not swung loosely on ropes, but only jammed up there tightly together, they wouldn't sound nearly as loud as they would do if they were pulled and rung properly. They jangled, more than rang.'

'They did the best they could,' said Diana soberly. 'I was awfully scared. I suppose the "enemy" didn't hear them because they were coming in the car, and must still have been some way away. I wonder if they would have come into the Hall if they *had* heard them.'

'Of course not,' said Roger. 'Clever bells – to warn us

but not them! I say – this is all very *peculiar*, isn't it? What's down that secret passage?'

'You mean *who* is,' said Diana. 'That man said "Where is *he*?" not "Where is *it*?" There's someone down there, doing something.'

'I don't know where, then,' said Roger. '*We* went right down to the brick wall, and there wasn't anyone. And, as far as I could see, there was absolutely no other passage or cave or anything. Just a tunnel.'

There was a silence. Everyone was thinking. 'Shall we go down the passage again some time and have another snoop?' asked Roger at last.

'No,' said everybody, very firmly. The idea of getting down there again at dead of night, with those bells nearby likely to ring all by themselves at any minute, didn't appeal to anyone.

'I tell you what we *could* do,' said Snubby suddenly. 'We could try and and find out where the *other* end of the secret passage is, and then explore it backwards, so to speak – to the other side of the brick wall.'

Everyone thought this was a very bright idea. Roger gave Snubby a little pat on the back. 'Now that *is* an idea,' he said. 'We might find something out then.'

'Yes – but wait a minute. We don't know where to look for the other end of the passage,' said Diana, after a moment's thought.

'We must go and ask Grandad again,' said Roger, promptly. 'Maybe he'll tell us this time.'

Diana suddenly yawned, and that set the others off. The church clock struck twelve, very solemnly indeed.

'We ought to go to bed,' said Diana. 'We'll never wake up in the morning. Where's old Barney going to sleep? He can't go back to Ring O' Bells Hall, that's certain.'

'I shouldn't think he wants to, either,' said Snubby. 'I know I wouldn't.'

'Well, I don't,' said Barney. 'Those bells rather shook me. I just can't understand it. Poor little Miranda is so frightened that she's not moved since I tucked her into my shirt. She must have had a fit when she heard them jangling out!'

'I had a pretty good fit myself,' said Snubby. 'Well, what about Barney. Couldn't he sleep here for the night? In this shed?'

'Yes – just for tonight,' said Roger, considering. 'I don't know if Miss Hannah would mind, but as we can't ask her now, we'll just say Barney *can* sleep here. After all, Miranda isn't likely to pop in through her window or anything.'

Barney was very tired. He arranged some sacks to lie on, and Diana found an old garden rug to cover him. 'We'll go in now,' she said. 'You'll be all right, Barney, won't you?'

'Fine,' said Barney, curling himself up. 'You go and get into bed – you'll be getting 'flu again, or something! See you tomorrow.'

'Yes – and we'll find the other end of the passage *some*how,' said Snubby. 'And down we'll go.'

'Though I expect we shall find the roof *has* fallen in, as that woman said,' remarked Roger, remembering.

'Anyway, we'll have a shot at finding it and exploring,' said Barney sleepily. 'Good night, all of you.'

Loony gave Barney one last lick on the nose and sniffed at the sleeping Miranda under his shirt. Then he trotted off quietly after the others. What an evening! He would have something to tell Loopy next day, no doubt about that!

Chapter Twenty

Grandad's Old Box

Neither Miss Pepper nor Miss Hannah had heard the bells ringing the night before. Diana didn't ask them straight out, but the children felt that they *had* to discover if they had been heard.

'I thought I heard bells ringing in the night,' Diana said casually at breakfast-time. 'Funny!'

'You must have been dreaming,' said Miss Pepper. 'Mustn't she, Hannah?'

'Yes – she probably heard the church clock striking,' said Miss Hannah. 'It has a lovely tone. Do you want a fourth sausage, Snubby?'

Snubby did. 'My appetite's coming back,' he informed Miss Hannah.

'*Coming* back!' she repeated horrified. 'You don't mean to say it's even worse than this?'

'He's just greedy – it's nothing to do with appetite,' said Diana. Snubby aimed a kick at her under the table, but Diana had already drawn her legs well out of the way, and there was a sudden agonised yelp from poor Loony. This meant Snubby getting hurriedly down from the table and crawling underneath to comfort him and apologise.

'*You'd* better have the last sausage, Roger, as Snubby had disappeared,' said Miss Pepper, whereupon Snubby came back again in a hurry.

'What are your plans today?' asked Miss Hannah. 'Riding? Walking? Lazing?'

'We thought we'd go and have a talk with Old Grandad

again,' said Diana. 'And then perhaps go for a walk. Do you want any errands done, Miss Hannah?'

'No, I don't think so,' said Miss Hannah. 'You'll do all your usual jobs first, I know – beds and so on.'

'Oh, of *course*,' said Diana. 'And you do know you've only got to ask us to do absolutely anything for you and we'll do it.'

'Like a shot,' said Snubby, finishing the last sausage. 'I do like the way you cook sausages, Miss Hannah – nice and *bursty*.'

'What extraordinary things you say, Snubby,' said Miss Hannah. 'Have you finished? Because if you have you might remove Loony from my feet. He's so heavy.'

Loony was removed, and Loopy followed. Diana got up to go and fetch Barney's tray of breakfast things. She had already been out to see him, and had taken him a very fine breakfast. Miranda was sitting licking marmalade off a piece of toast. She offered it to Diana.

'No thanks, darling Miranda,' said Diana. 'You can have it all. I don't want even one lick. Barney, we'll come out as soon as we can. We've got a few things to do.'

'Right,' said Barney. 'I'm going to mend that bit of fence that's broken. I must do *some*thing in return for my breakfast!'

'Oh – Miss Hannah *will* be pleased,' said Diana. That was so like Barney. He always felt he simply must repay any kindness as soon as ever he could.

About eleven o'clock the four children, Loony, Loopy and Miranda were all going up the lane to Hubbard Cottage. They stopped at a little shop to buy a tin of tobacco for the old man they were going to see. The woman knew quite well what he smoked, which was lucky.

They walked up to the front door of the cottage and knocked.

'Come away in!' called Mother Hubbard's voice, and

in they went. Mother Hubbard was there, scrubbing her floor. She was pleased to see the children. She got up, wiping her hands, and smiled at them.

'Could we see Old Grandad?' asked Diana politely. 'We've brought him a little tin of tobacco.'

'Well, if that isn't kind of you!' said the old lady, and she took the tin. 'I wish you *could* see him – but he's got one of his poorly turns and he's in bed.'

'Oh,' said the children, and looked so disappointed that Mother Hubbard felt sorry.

'There's nothing *I* can tell you or do for you instead, is there?' she asked.

'Well,' said Diana, and paused. She looked at the others and they nodded. 'You see, it's like this – Old Grandad told us about some old books he once had, and we wondered if he still had them and would lend them to us.'

'Old books?' said Mother Hubbard, frowning as she tried to remember. 'Let me see – those must have been thrown away years since.'

'Oh – *what* a pity!' said Diana, disappointed.

'When I came to look after Old Grandad, he had a wonderful lot of rubbish,' said Mother Hubbard. 'And I had a good turn-out and threw a lot away. But I did put some into an old box of his. You can rummage through that if you like, and see if you can find any old books there. He wouldn't mind!'

'Oh, *could* we!' said Diana delighted. 'We'd love to. We're so interested in Ring O' Bells Village, you know.'

'Yes – it's a strange old place,' said Mother Hubbard. 'Do you know what Old Grandad said to me this morning? He said he heard the bells at the old Hall ringing last night. The things he do think! Why those bells haven't rung for years – they've got no ropes to pull them with.'

'Didn't you hear the bells too?' asked Roger.

'I sleep sound,' said Mother Hubbard. 'And if I heard bells ringing at Ring O' Bells Hall, I'd think I was off my head. Will you believe it, when Fanny Tapp came by this morning, and I told her what Old Grandad said, she made out she'd heard them too, and was proper scared in the night. The tales some folks make up!'

The children listened to all this and said nothing. So others had heard the bells too!

'You come along into my washhouse,' said Mother Hubbard. 'I've got Grandad's box there. And would you like some of my gingers? I made them yesterday.'

The 'gingers' turned out to be nice, hard, ginger biscuits, almost as good as Naomi Barlow's cinnamon biscuits. The children followed Mother Hubbard into the little washhouse, munching the biscuits.

There were shelves round the washhouse and Mother Hubbard pointed to an old brass-bound box. 'That's Grandad's,' she said. 'Can you lift it down?'

'Yes, thank you,' said Barney, and lifted it down. It wasn't very heavy, so there couldn't be much in it.

A loud call came from the little front garden and Mother Hubbard hurried off. 'That's the baker,' she said. 'You undo the box and see what you can find. If there's books there, you can borrow them.'

The children opened the box. It had a simple catch to fasten it. They bent over the open box, excited. What would they find?

They found very little. There were a few roughly carved wooden figures, which probably Old Grandad had done himself and was proud of. There was a funny old ship, its sails in rags, its mast broken. There was an old wooden pipe, and what looked like a home-made whistle.

'Not much here,' said Roger. 'Wait – here's a book!'

He took it out. It was bound in leather that was warped and discoloured with damp. Many of the pages had stuck together. The children pored over it, trying to pull the pages apart.

'Be careful – you'll tear them,' said Roger. 'Blow! This book is in that difficult old lettering. We can't possibly make out much – and look how messed up the pages are – we can hardly read anything anyhow.'

They all pored over the book, trying to make out a word here and there. They couldn't even find out the title. It was in flourishing letters, so decorative that the children couldn't read them.

'No good,' said Roger, disappointed. 'Still – if Mother Hubbard will let us, we'll borrow it, just in *case* we can make out something. Though how we could ever find out if the secret passage is mentioned here I simply don't know!'

'Found anything interesting?' asked Mother Hubbard, appearing again. 'Nothing but rubbish there, I expect. Oh, you've got an old book. Borrow it, if you like.'

'Thank you,' said Diana. 'We'd like to. I hope Old Grandad will be better soon.'

'I'll tell him you've been, and give him the tobacco,' said Mother Hubbard. 'Goodbye – and keep the book as long as you like.'

They all went out. Barney took Miranda out from his jacket. He had hidden her there in case Mother Hubbard or Old Grandad didn't like monkeys. She had been as good as gold. The two dogs, each with a bone from the old lady, welcomed the children as if they had been away for a week. Roger laughed and untied them.

'Old Grandad doesn't like dogs,' he told them, 'so don't bark your heads off like that, or he'll come after you with a stick!'

They went to the village for an ice cream. Snubby was carrying the book, dipping into it as he went. He suddenly stood still and said 'HA!' in a most excited voice.

'What are you ha-ing about?' asked Diana. 'Found a recipe for cooking sausages or something?'

'Look at this,' said Snubby, and the others crowded round to see. Snubby had got the book open at the very last page. He pointed to the inside of the back cover.

'There's a kind of pocket there,' he said. 'And there's something in it – a map – a map, I should think. Let's sit down somewhere and find out.'

They went into a field and sat down. The dogs ran off to the rabbit-holes, delighted. Miranda went with them – not to look for rabbits, but to jeer at the two digging dogs!

Snubby drew out a paper from the old pocket inside the back cover of the book. 'It's parchment,' he said. 'Gosh, I hope it doesn't fall to pieces in my hand!'

'Give it to me,' said Diana. 'I'm more careful than you are.'

With deft, gentle fingers she unfolded the parchment, and spread it on her lap.

It had been folded in four, and the folds were already cracking.

'It's a map!' said Diana, thrilled. 'Look – a map of Ring O' Bells Hall! Oh, if only it would show the secret passage!'

They all pored over it in excitement. The map was not so discoloured and faded as the pages of the book, and the children could easily make out the name at the bottom. 'Dourley. Ring O' Bells Hall.'

'It's genuine!' said Roger. 'Now we really *may* find out something!'

Chapter Twenty-One

A Little Hunting Around

They did find out something. They found out quite a lot. It might be difficult to decipher the old printing on the pages of the book – but it was much easier to read a plan or map.

It seemed to be a plan of Ring O' Bells Hall, showing all the ground floor. The two towers were indicated, one as a square, one as a circle at each end of the Hall. Bells were drawn in the square showing that that was the Bell Tower.

'Where's the little panelled room where the secret passage begins?' said Roger.

'Here,' said Diana, and pointed to it. 'That must be it – it's off the hall, and near the kitchen and it's small.'

'Is the secret passage shown?' asked Snubby, bending his head over the map.

'No,' said Diana, in disappointment.

'There's a letter P in the room,' said Roger, pointing. 'Why? P for passage, of course. It *is* a P, isn't it?'

They all agreed that it was. But the P only told them what they already knew – that there was a passage leading off the little panelled room!

'Well – it's a thrilling old map, and beautifully drawn – but it doesn't tell us what we want to know,' said Roger, in disappointment. 'I suppose there isn't anything else in the old pocket inside the back cover, Di?'

Diana looked, inserting her fingers gently. She gave a little exclamation. 'Yes – I believe there is!'

Very slowly and carefully she drew out another piece

of parchment, much smaller than the other. It was folded in half. With fingers that suddenly shook, she opened it. Everyone bent over it at once.

At first they couldn't make it out. It seemed to be merely the plan of some bit of countryside. Then Snubby's rather dirty finger poked down at the paper.

'P!' he said. 'P again. P for passage. Look, it begins here, by this house, or whatever it is.'

'I should think it's meant to be Ring O' Bells Hall,' said Diana. 'It's roughly the shape – you know how it sticks out at the back, so to speak. Well, all right – we'll say that P is for Passage – the secret passage. How does that help us?'

'Can't you *see*?' said Snubby impatiently and he jabbed at the map again. 'There's a faded red line leading from that P – look, there it goes – right from Ring O' Bells Hall, over the stream, through the wood – and ends at this other P here!'

'Gosh – you're right, Snubby!' said Roger. 'It *is* the *passage* – must be! But it doesn't go over the stream, of course – it goes under – and under the wood – and it seems to end at some little building, if that's what this square indicates.'

'What building would that be?' said Diana, thinking. 'Could it be – Ring O' Bells Cottage?'

'It could be – and is!' cried Roger. 'Of course, of course. Don't you remember what Old Grandad kept saying, when we asked him where the secret passage went to. "Ask Mother Barlow, ask Mother Barlow!" It went to her cottage, of course, that's why we had to ask her – though she's been dead for ages. He'd forgotten that.'

'And Naomi Barlow lives there now,' said Diana. 'I wonder if *she* knows anything about it. But I say – where in the world does the secret passage end in her cottage? Don't you remember the solid stone floor in each of the rooms? There didn't seem anywhere for a passage to open.'

'There wasn't,' said Snubby. 'I'd stake anything that no passage is under the floors of Ring O' Bells Cottage.'

'Yet this old map certainly shows the passage ending there,' said Roger, puzzled. 'Perhaps it ends somewhere nearby – in the wood, under a trapdoor, or something like that.'

'Yes – that might be so,' said Barney. 'Anyway, we know the way the passage takes now – it runs from the panelled room we know, avoids the house, goes straight under the garden, runs to this stream, goes under it – must be pretty deep there, I should think, or the water would seep through – then under the wood, and up to the cottage, ending somewhere about there.'

'Gosh – it's wonderful!' said Snubby, too thrilled for words. 'What do we do next?'

'I'll tell you what we do next,' said Diana, a marvellous idea suddenly filling her mind. 'We go to Ring O' Bells Cottage, and ask Naomi Barlow if she'd be kind enough to let Barney sleep in her little store-room, with Miranda – because we can't find a place for him in the village!'

'And he can snoop round, and ask her questions and see if he can find the passage!' said Snubby. 'What a brainwave!'

'She loved Miranda – she would say yes, I'm sure,' said Diana. 'Let's go and ask her immediately after lunch.'

Feeling very thrilled indeed, they all went home to enjoy a good lunch. Barney had his out in the garden with Miranda, who spent a most enjoyable half-hour peeling the skin off a tomato and eating it.

After lunch they set off for Ring O' Bells Cottage. They were almost there when they saw Naomi Barlow hurrying along, looking like old Red Riding Hood again, because she had on the red cloak! She greeted them kindly.

'I hope you weren't going to see me, children. I am going down to clean out the church, and shan't be back till six.'

'We *were* going to see you,' said Diana, disappointed. 'We were going to tell you that we simply can't find *any*where in the village for poor Barney and his monkey to sleep in at night – and Miss Hannah won't have him because she's afraid of monkeys. So we wondered, we just wondered if – '

'I'd let him sleep in my little old cottage!' finished Naomi, and she smiled. 'Of course he can – he can have the room where *I* used to sleep for years when I was a child. You remember the store-room I showed you? He can sleep there – and I shall have a pet monkey to fuss over again.'

'Thank you, Mam, very much indeed,' said Barney gratefully.

'You go up to the cottage now, and set the store-room to rights,' said Naomi. 'Tidy it up, and put down the old mattress you'll see in one corner. That'll save me doing it when I come back tired.'

'You *are* kind,' said Diana. 'We'll love to do that – and is there any job you'd like us to do for *you* – clean the windows, or anything?'

'Oh, no – the only other things you can do is to help yourselves to my cinnamon biscuits!' said old Naomi with a laugh. 'They're in that big tin on the mantelpiece. Now I must hurry. You go along to my cottage – you'll find the door isn't locked.'

She hurried off, looking more like an old Red Riding Hood than ever. The children looked at each other in delight. Could anything be better! A bed and shelter for

Barney and Miranda in the very place where the other end of the secret passage began!

'We're in luck's way,' said Diana, as they turned down the little path to Naomi's cottage.

'Yes – we can have a good look at the floors in each room to make sure there's no passage below,' said Roger. 'I wish we could do something in return for the old woman's kindness.'

'I shall pick some bluebells and put them about the cottage,' said Diana, and she went to pick a big bunch. The boys went on with the dogs, Miranda on Snubby's shoulder for a change.

They came to the cottage. The door was not locked, and they opened it and went in. 'Let's have a good look round first,' said Roger. They were examining the kitchen floor when Diana came in with her bluebells.

'Found anything?' she asked, putting the flowers into a jug, and looking round for some water. She found some in a pail. There were no taps, of course, because Naomi had to draw her water from the well outside.

'Look at this floor,' said Roger. He was on his knees, examining it closely. 'I could bet anything that these stone flags haven't been disturbed for hundreds of years! You can't shift a single one. They're set so close together too. If there *is* a passage underneath, it can't be got at by us, that's certain.'

The floors were the same in every room, solid and firm, though uneven. The stones were hollowed where much treading had been done. 'Shows how old they are,' said Roger, marvelling.

They went into the store-room and tidied it for Barney. 'It smells nice,' he said, sniffing at the pickle jars and jam. I shall like sleeping here. I shall dream of dinner with pickles, and tea with jam!'

They found the old mattress, and put it on the floor.

There really wasn't much room for anything else then. It was just a cupboard of a room, but Barney was not at all particular.

'Well, that's done,' said Diana. 'Now what about having a good look round the garden and in the wood nearby, just to see if we *can* find anything else – an old stone trapdoor, or something – hidden under grass, perhaps.'

They went out into the sunshine. First they searched the little garden, but there was obviously nothing there. Then they went out of the gate, separated, and examined every inch of the ground all round the garden. But there was nothing to be found there either.

'It's maddening,' said Diana. 'The entrance *must* be somewhere. Barney, you must get into conversation with Naomi Barlow tonight, and see if *she* knows anything. It's so long since the passage was used, apparently, that people seem to have forgotten all about it. But she may have learnt something from Mother Barlow.'

'Right. I'll do my best,' said Barney. 'Now what about one of those cinnamon biscuits?'

'Oh, yes,' said Snubby and lifted down the tin. They each took one and put the tin back, though Loony and Loopy clamoured for one too.

'Certainly not,' said Snubby firmly. 'You were not included in the invitation to help yourselves to biscuits. Anyway, you've had a wonderful afternoon, scrabbling round the wood.'

'Let's go back to tea now,' said Diana. 'I'm hungry.'

So back they went to one of Miss Hannah's good teas. How they hoped that Barney would be able to find out something from old Naomi Barlow!

Chapter Twenty-Two

Barney Has An Idea

The four met the next morning in the garden at Miss Hannah's. Snubby had Barney's breakfast tray all ready, and he carried it out, with Roger and Diana running in front to greet Barney and Miranda.

'Did you find out anything?' asked Diana eagerly. 'Did Naomi tell you where the passage began?'

'No, she wouldn't,' said Barney. 'At first she said she knew nothing about it all – the passage was known only to a very few at any time, and those were the Dourlays themselves. Then she said it wasn't in existence now as far as she knew.'

'Blow!' said Roger. 'Not at all helpful. Didn't she *really* know anything?'

'Well, it was strange,' said Barney slowly, 'when I tried to press her a bit about it, because I couldn't help feeling that she knew more than she said, she got all upset, and said something rather peculiar.'

'What?' asked everyone at once.

'She said, "I'd forgotten the drowning for years, and now you've made me think of it. I shall have my nightmares again. I tell you that passage has never been used since the drowning. It's gone, it's gone!" '

The children listened to this in astonished silence. What could it all mean?

'What drowning?' wondered Diana. 'And why hasn't the passage been used since the *drowning*? Whatever has it got to do with somebody being drowned? You can't drown in a passage.'

'There's just one explanation,' said Barney and he lowered his voice. 'It may be wrong, but it's the only one I can think of. Where do you drown? In water. And where is there any water near Naomi's Cottage? Only in the well.'

There was a pause. 'I still don't see any explanation,' said Roger. 'What do you mean?'

'I mean this,' said Barney, 'and it may sound farfetched, but I think it's worth going into. Suppose that secret passage has its outlet in old Naomi's *well*? And somebody, who was being chased, used that passage and instead of being able to get out of the well, fell down and was drowned? If it had happened when Naomi was very young, and she heard of it, she would never forget it. It would give her nightmares. Maybe even the story of it, if told to her as a child, would be enough to make her dream.'

'I think you're right,' said Roger. 'It all fits together. But good gracious – how could a secret passage open into a well?'

'I don't know,' said Barney. 'That's for us to find out. If there *is* an opening down that well – and we all know how very deep it is – there must be some way of getting up or down it – some footholds of some kind – iron staples driven into the wall, perhaps. We could soon find out.'

'This is very, very exciting,' said Snubby, rubbing his hands together. 'We'll have to be careful not to miss our footing, though – or there'd be a nasty splash!'

'Don't say things like that,' said Diana with a shiver.

An impatient voice suddenly called from the house. 'Children! Whatever are you doing? Are you *never* coming to breakfast?'

'Good gracious – we forgot all about it,' said Roger in surprise. 'Fancy *you* forgetting too, Snubby. Unbelievable!'

'We'll be out as soon as we can, Barney,' said Diana, and the three of them tore in with the dogs at their heels.

They all had to go riding that morning, because they had arranged it the day before. Barney went too, wearing old jodhpurs belonging to Miss Hannah's nephew, who was now grown up and gone away. He was a perfect horseman, having been trained to the saddle from his babyhood. The children admired him as he rode. Good old Barney, he was a marvel!

As they rode, he told them about his night at Ring O' Bells Cottage. 'I slept in that tiny room,' he said, 'and I dreamt of food all night long, the smells were so delicious. Snubby, you ought to try taking a few pickle jars and spice jars to your bedroom. You'd have wonderful dreams. You'd probably be eating all night long in them.'

Everyone laughed. Snubby considered the idea seriously and thought it a very good one. He debated whether to subtract a few bottles and jars from Miss Hannah's larder and give the idea a trail.

Nobody noticed the scenery very much that morning because they were so excited at the idea of examining the well.

They talked and talked about it, and at lunch that day Diana could hardly eat anything, she felt so full of anticipation. However, neither Roger nor Snubby were in the least affected, so the lunch was not wasted.

That afternoon they all went up to Ring O' Bells Cottage with Barney. 'Old Naomi is going off to finish cleaning the church,' he said. 'It would be a good chance for us to have a look at the well.'

The cottage was empty when they arrived. Naomi had gone. The children made sure of this and then went straight to the well. They looked down.

It certainly *was* a very deep well. Roger dropped a

139

stone down again and the listened for the splash, which seemed to be a very long time coming.

'There it is,' said Barney at last. 'Now, let's look for a way down.'

The little ferns grew so thickly in the well walls that it was difficult to see even the bricks. Barney felt about, leaning over the well side. Diana held on to him, scared of his falling down.

'I've got something!' said Barney at last. 'There's a kind of iron loop here. Wait – I'll pull out these ferns.'

He pulled them out and then the others could see what he meant. A loop of iron was fixed to the wall. It seemed very firmly fastened in. Barney gave it a tug.

'Well – if this is a foothold to use when going down, there should be others in a row down the wall. I'm going over to see.'

'Oh, Barney – don't,' said Diana.

'I'll get a rope from the store-room and tie it round Barney's waist,' said Roger, who also didn't like the idea of Barney going down the well. 'We'll tie the rope to the well post, and hold on to it ourselves, letting Barney down bit by bit, as he finds something to hold on to.'

They got the rope and Barney let them tie him. Secretly he considered this rather silly, for he was a first-rate acrobat and climber – but he could see that Diana was very scared.

He went over the side, treading on the iron loop he had found. He put his foot down cautiously and felt about among the ferns. He found another loop!

'Got it!' he called back cheerfully to the others. 'This must be the right way down. No wonder nobody knew of it, it's so well-hidden by the ferns.'

Ferns did not grow very far down, however. Barney found it easier to feel the iron loops after a time. One or two of them fell away as he trod on them and gave him a little shock. The others heard them splashing into the water, and held very tightly to Barney's rope. Diana's heart beat fast. Oh, dear – this was very dangerous! Surely they ought not to do it? But they must find out, they must!

Barney went down a very long way. 'Can you see the water yet?' yelled Roger, his voice sounding most peculiar down the well.

'Yes – just,' called back Barney. 'I say – I can't feel any more loops for my feet. Blow – don't say the rest of them have rotted and fallen away!'

He felt about again, shivering, for it was icy-cold in the dank, dark well. No – there were no footholds at all below where he was. He called up to Roger.

'Roger! I've not got a torch with me. Tie yours carefully on a bit of string and let it down. I want to see if the entrance to the passage is anywhere here, as there aren't any more footholds.'

The torch came down, twisting round and round on its string. It only just reached Barney! He took it and switched it on. Ah – now he could see!

He sent up such a yell that the others nearly let go of the rope. Miranda, who hadn't gone down the well with Barney, looked down into the darkness anxiously.

'What is it?' shouted Roger, his voice echoing all the way down.

'There's a hole here, right in the side of the well!' called Barney. 'I bet it's the entrance to the secret passage! I say – what a marvellous idea to have a way of escape leading to a well. Nobody would ever dream of that! I'm going in!'

'No, no!' almost shrieked Snubby. 'Wait. We want to come too!'

'Not Diana,' came back Barney's voice.

'I don't want to come!' cried Diana. 'Anyway, someone

must guide the rope and hold it as you each go down. I'll do that.'

Barney stepped into the black hole, flashing his torch. He could see nothing but a tunnel underground. Gosh – this was exciting! They really had found the other end of the secret passage now. Would it lead back to Ring O' Bells Hall, as it showed on the map?

Roger came down next, feeling for the loops with his feet, and holding on to others with his hands. Then Snubby, who left a frenzied Loony behind. Diana had a job to stop Loony and Loopy from leaping into the well.

Soon all three boys were standing in the narrow hole. It was merely a round gap in the brickwork of the well. Did the water ever reach as high as that? Probably not. The spring from which the well water came must be very deep under the earth indeed.

'You can see what old Naomi means by someone drowning now, can't you?' said Barney. 'Probably some-one came hurrying along this tunnel in the dark and didn't realise he'd come to the end. He must have run straight out of the hole and dropped down into the well.'

'Horrible!' said Roger, shivering with excitement, cold and horror. 'Come on. Let's explore the tunnel. But hadn't we better keep quiet, in case there's somebody else about? There may be someone down the tunnel at the other end!'

'Yes. Keep quiet then,' whispered Barney. 'Come along. I'll use my torch, and you can follow.'

So down the weird tunnel they went, following each other in the darkness. What a strange adventure!

Chapter Twenty-Three

Underground

For some way the tunnel ran straight and level. The roof was low in places and the boys bumped their heads till they got used to looking out for a sudden dip in the roof. They trailed on, with only the light of Barney's torch. The tunnel smelt dank and musty, and Roger hoped the air was good enough. If it was bad they might faint and fall down!

'Just as well we left Di behind to raise the alarm if we don't get back,' he thought.

The tunnel took a sharp bend, and ran downwards instead of level. The boys went on steadily. They all wished they had warm coats on, for they felt very chilly indeed. Suddenly Barney stopped and pointed with his torch to something.

A tree-root had penetrated through the roof of the tunnel and hung down in front of them! It looked very strange.

'We're under the trees now,' said Barney in a whisper.

'We shall soon leave the wood behind and come to the stream. I bet the tunnel takes a big dip under that, to get away from the damp river-bed!'

It did. It suddenly went down very steeply indeed, and became wet and muddy. The roof dripped water. Barney shone his torch on it. 'Look,' he said. 'Someone reinforced the roof just there with great stones. They've made a kind of stone arch. A good thing too, or the roof would have crumbled very quickly.'

They went on again, and then came to a full stop.

'Blow! said Barney, shining his torch in front of him. 'The roof *has* fallen in here – look!'

So it had. A great mass of rubble lay in front of them, and there was a broken hole in the roof.

'It might not be very serious,' said Roger. 'Let's just scrabble a bit and see if we can get through.'

It was difficult to 'scrabble' with only their hands, but they soon found that Roger was right – the fall was only trivial. They could make a way through at one side, by piling the earth and stones in the middle of the fall.

They went on again. Then Barney spoke in a low whisper, almost in Roger's ear. 'We must be getting somewhere near Ring O' Bells now – better be very cautious.'

The tunnel now began to slant upwards a little, and curved to the right. Then another roof-fall stopped them. This time it was a bigger one. The three looked at it in silence.

Then, from behind the roof-fall came a noise – a spasmodic noise of quick, regular sounds, painful to hear – the noise that Barney had heard, distorted and muffled by distance and by the fact that it had come up the secret passage to the little panelled room. No wonder Barney hadn't recognised the noise.

It was very simple to recognise now that it was near – just the other side of the roof-fall. It was a man coughing painfully – cough, cough, cough, – pause – cough, cough, cough – pause – cough, cough.

Then there was a dreadful groan, and the man on the other side of the roof-fall muttered something in a broken voice.

'He's terribly ill, I should think,' whispered Barney. 'He ought to have a doctor. What's he doing down here, do you suppose?'

'Kidnapped, probably,' said Roger, also in a whisper. 'As for a doctor – that's probably who we saw when we hid in the chest the other night – do you remember the man with a small bag? He was probably a doctor called in by the woman.'

'But wouldn't a doctor be amazed to be taken to a patient hidden down here?' asked Snubby.

'He's probably a doctor who attends the gang or whatever it is that kidnaps people and hides them here,' said Barney.

'Look,' said Roger, straightening himself up. He had been bending down, peeping here and there. 'Look – there's a little space in this mass of rubble – you can see right through it.'

Barney bent down and put his eye to the space. He could make out part of the clothed body of a man, tossing and turning. He could not see his face.

'Shall I speak to him and ask him who he is?' whispered Barney. The others nodded. They felt sure the man was a captive, a prisoner, probably kidnapped and held for some reason or other.

Barney spoke through the hole. 'Hallo, there! Who are you?'

The man beyond stopped moving at once. He now appeared to be sitting up.

'Who spoke?' he whispered, in a croaking, frightened voice. 'Who is it?'

'Never mind,' said Barney. 'Tell us who you are. What are you doing here?'

'I've been kidnapped,' groaned the man. 'I'm a detective, and I've been spying on a gang who are known to be kidnappers. They've got *me* now – and now they want to get out of me all I know – then they'll bump me off. So I'm not telling.'

He fell back and began to cough again, a dreadful tearing cough. The boys knew he must be very ill. They didn't doubt his word at all.

'Shall we try and get through to you, sir, and – get you out this way?' asked Barney, realising as he said it that it would be quite impossible to get such an ill man along the tunnel and up the sides of the well.

'No. No, I can't even stand,' said the man, beginning to cough again. 'Listen – they'll kill me if they think I've been talking to anyone, so be careful. Listen to what I say.'

'We're listening,' said Barney.

'Three of the gang are coming here tonight to try and get out of me, for the last time, all that I know about them and others,' said the man hoarsely. 'They'll be here at eleven. Can you hide till they come, and then warn the police? Tell them its Detective Inspector Rawlings who's sending the message.'

'Right – and then if the three are down here in the secret passage, they'll be nicely rounded up,' said Barney, seeing it all. 'A very good plan, sir.'

'Does the caretaker-woman feed you?' asked Roger, through the hole. 'Is she in it too?'

'Everyone's in it!' said the man. 'I knew they were using this place for their headquarters, but I'd no idea there was any secret passage here. There's many a poor fellow's been put down here!'

He coughed so badly that he couldn't stop. Barney and Roger and Snubby felt distressed. 'If only we could get to him to help him – but this wretched roof-fall is too big to shift without tools,' said Barney. He called through the hole in a pause between the coughs.

'We're going now, sir, but we'll do exactly as you say. Goodbye!'

They made their way carefully back, clambering over the side of the other roof-fall when they came to it. They were at last beside the well, and heard Diana calling in a despairing voice.

'Barney! Roger! Snubby! Oh, do come back! Roger, what's happened?'

'Poor old Diana!' said Roger, suddenly realising what a long time they had been, and how scared Diana must be. He yelled up.

'Hallo, Di! We're back all safe and sound, with news for you!'

'Thank goodness!' came Diana's voice, sounding very tearful.

Barney felt for the rope end hanging down the well and tied it round his waist in case he fell. 'I'm coming up. Diana!' he called.

He was soon up, going hand over hand up the well wall, climbing like a cat. Miranda leapt chattering on to his shoulder as soon as he appeared, fondling and caressing him lovingly. Loony and Loopy threw themselves on him barking.

'I feel like doing that myself, Barney,' said Diana, with tears of relief in her eyes. 'You *have* been gone a long time.'

'We'll get Roger and Snubby up and then tell you our news,' said Barney, and he turned to look down the well. Snubby was already coming up. Roger soon followed. All three shivered with the cold, and were glad to feel the hot May sun on their shoulders.

They told the astonished Diana all that had happened. She could hardly believe her ears.

'*Well*! To think that kidnappers use the old Ring O' Bells Hall like that! I suppose that's why that woman put in for the job and got it – it would be easy for any gang to get in and out, and use the secret passage for hiding things and people in, if they had someone actually here all the time, watching over their prisoners, ready to let the gang in and out of the place!' Diana paused for breath.

'Yes – no one would ever guess that an old show-place

like that in a country village would be such a cunning headquarters,' said Roger. 'One of the gang must, of course, have heard about that secret passage and seen its possibilities. And to think that no one could go down there because the woman was always on guard!'

'There's one thing I don't understand,' said Barney. 'We went down that passage, but we came to a brick wall, bricking it up. There was no one there then, yet I heard that man coughing the night before. Where was he?'

They all thought hard. 'All I can say is that some of the bricks in the wall must be easily removable,' said Roger, at last. 'After all, we didn't examine the wall very closely. It must be possible to take out enough bricks to get through. I'm sure we shall find that's right. It's all very clever and very well planned.'

'It's a bad look-out for that detective tonight,' said Snubby. 'He won't tell what he knows, that's certain – so they'll either bump him off, or leave him there to die. He's ill enough to pop off at any time, I should think.'

'So should I be, down in that cold, dank, damp, chilly place, shut up day and night with no air to breathe,' said Barney. He sat on the wall that ran round the old well, and thought for a minute or two.

'I'm seeing a lot of things now,' he said. 'You know when I got a lift in that van which took me to Lillinghame, but which I saw later on, outside Ring O' Bells Hall, late at night? Well, there was something in that van which terrified Miranda when she got into it. All *I* could see was a sort of white thing that seemed to run about on the floor of the van – but it was probably the detective's hand out of its covers! I expect he was lying there under sacks and things, probably doped with something.'

'Yes – it looks as if the prisoner was brought here that night,' said Snubby. 'Poor wretch! What a long time to spend down there.'

'We must make our plans now,' said Barney. 'And – we must make them very, very carefully.'

Chapter Twenty-Four

That Night

They did make their plans carefully. They talked everything over bit by bit, and discussed exactly what would be best to do.

'No good saying a word to Miss Pepper,' said Roger. 'She would be scared, go to the police, and they'd do exactly what the detective doesn't want – go in immediately to rescue him, and then that woman would warn the gang, they wouldn't come tonight, and not one of them would be captured.'

'For that same reason I think it would be best to stick to what the man said, and not warn the police till the gang are actually down the passage,' said Barney. 'The police might act too soon.'

'All the same, I think the poor ill man ought to be taken up immediately,' said tender-hearted Diana. 'He might die.'

'I don't think another few hours would hurt him – and he'd be pretty wild if he thought we hadn't done what he told us to,' said Roger. 'No – I think we must do exactly what he said – wait till the gang is there, and then rush for the police station.'

'Where are we going to watch for the gang to come?' asked Snubby. 'In Ring O' Bells Hall?'

'Yes,' said Barney. 'We might be spotted, anywhere outside. You never know. There are plenty of good hiding-places inside. Those chests, for instance.'

'I don't like those,' said Snubby. 'I feel sort of cooped up there.'

'Right. We'll find somewhere else then,' said Barney.

'But listen – we don't take Loony. If he growls he'll certainly give us away again.'

Loony heard his name and ran up at once, wagging his tail violently. Snubby patted the silky black head. 'All right,' he said reluctantly. 'We won't take him. But he'll howl like anything.'

'Well, he'll have to,' said Barney. 'This is too serious a matter to spoil for the sake of taking Loony.'

'What about Miranda?' asked Diana. 'She gibbered like anything the other night.'

'She'll be all right tonight,' said Barney. 'I'll put her collar on, and a lead, so that she has to stay on my shoulder. I will see she doesn't utter a sound.'

'All right. We hide, and we wait, and we watch to make sure the gang are safely down the secret passage,' said Roger. 'Then we rush and get the police in – is that right? Suppose they don't believe us?'

'They will if we say the detective's name,' said Barney. 'Detective Inspector Rawlings – they'll know about him and will have been informed that he has disappeared. Anyway, I'll jolly well *make* them believe us.'

'Those bells knew what they were doing all right, when they rang themselves the other night,' said Snubby suddenly. 'Talk about enemies! I'm not awfully looking forward to waiting in Ring O' Bells Hall tonight, I don't mind telling you. I'm scared of those bells.'

'Well, don't come then,' said Barney. 'Stay with Diana. I'm not letting her come.'

Diana was relieved. She had thought she really *ought* to come, but she didn't want to in the least. If Barney said she wasn't to, well, that was that. She would stay at home with Loony – and Snubby too, perhaps.

No – Snubby was going, whether he was scared of the bells or not. 'You can't keep *me* out of it,' he said, putting on a most courageous voice. 'I may not want to come very much, but I'm jolly well coming, all the same!'

'Good for you,' said Barney. 'Where's the police station? We'd better know all these details – the shortest way to get to it from Ring O' Bells Hall, and all that. Pity we can't telephone them – but they'd probably think it was a spoof call. Anyway I don't remember seeing telephone wires anywhere near the Hall.'

'What time shall we be there?' said Roger. 'The detective said the gang would arrive at eleven. We'd better be there at ten, and watch out for them. We shall have plenty of time to arrange our hiding-places.'

'Yes – ten o'clock,' agreed Barney. 'Gosh – this is all frightfully exciting, isn't it? I never thought anything like this would happen when I popped down here to see you for a few days.'

'Excitement must be very good for 'flu,' said Diana. 'I feel perfectly all right now. I bet Snubby still thinks of his poor wobbly legs though!'

'I do not!' said Snubby indignantly. 'Except that I keep feeling awful pangs of hunger all day long, I'm just exactly the same as usual.'

'I thought you *usually* felt pangs of hunger,' began Diana, and then was interrupted by Roger, who had just looked at his watch.

'Wheee-ew! I say! It's half-past five! Would you believe it? We've missed tea at Miss Hannah's now. It will be all cleared away when we get there. What shall we do?'

'No wonder Snubby began talking about pangs of hunger,' said Barney. 'I'm feeling some myself.'

'Let's go down to that village shop and see if they'll give us something,' said Diana. 'We could at least get ice creams. I do hope Miss Hannah won't be too wild with us.'

They found the shop open and were able to buy buns,

ice creams, chocolate and orangeade, so they didn't do too badly. The dogs had an ice cream each too, for being so good and patient all the afternoon. Miranda had half of one, because Barney said they sometimes gave her a tummy-ache and he didn't want her whining that evening!

They went back to Miss Hannah's. Barney went too. He planned to wait in the shed till the time came for him to join the others and go to Ring O' Bells Hall. He would have supper with them first.

'It's such a wonderful evening perhaps we could have a sort of picnic supper out in the garden,' suggested Diana. 'I believe it's all cold tonight.'

It was – so they were allowed to take their plates into the garden and sit on the grass, with Loony and Loopy and Miranda greedily watching every mouthful. Miranda was too clever at snatching, and Barney had to speak to her very severly. She hid her face in his neck and made little mournful noises. Diana wanted to fuss over and pet her, but Barney wouldn't let her.

'No Diana. She's getting spoilt with all the fuss everyone makes of her. A scolding will do her good. Do you know, at Naomi's last night she actually went to a bottle of cherries, took the lid off – unscrewed it, mind you – and began to take out cherries with her paw. And Naomi let her! No wonder she's getting spoilt.'

'She's such a darling, though. I do so love her,' said Diana. Loony was immediately jealous and came and put his head on her knee, looking up at her mournfully out of melting brown eyes.

'Go on with you!' said Diana, tapping his nose with her spoon. 'It's cupboard love! You want a bit of my blancmange.'

Loony looked at her, got up and trotted indoors. He came out with Miss Hannah's lovely green bathtowel, treading on it as he ran, and tripping himself up. He put it down at Diana's feet, as if to say, 'You're not very kind to me – but look what I do for you!'

'You're very naughty,' said Diana. 'Now I've got to get up and put it back again. No, Loopy, no – you are *not* to feel you've to play a silly trick too. If you dare to go in and bring out the hall mats I'll SMACK you!'

They almost forgot what was going to happen that evening as they had their picnic supper and played about with the dogs and Miranda.

Miss Hannah and Miss Pepper watched them through the window. They were having their own supper in peace. 'How nice to be young and carefree like that!' said Miss Hannah. 'No worries, no serious cares – just able to pop into bed and shut their eyes and sleep till morning without a single worrying thought.'

She would have been amazed if she had known the worries and cares the children had that night. They were certainly not going to be able to go to sleep with no worries till the morning. Snubby, in fact, felt that his life was full of fears and worries as the evening drew on!

'Snubby, you're looking tired,' said Miss Pepper, seeing a worried frown on his face. 'You'd better pop off to bed straight away.'

'Right,' said Snubby, thinking that he might as well get two hours or so of sleep before he had to face the darkness and silence of Ring O' Bells Hall. He went up in such a docile manner that Miss Pepper was most surprised, and a little alarmed. Surely Snubby was not sickening for something else?

Nobody was late that night. Barney said good night and went out of the gate, presumably to go to Naomi's. He slipped back through the hedge at the bottom of the garden, and made his way to the shed with Miranda. He settled himself quietly on some sacks to await the striking of the church clock. They were all to set off at ten.

154

Snubby fell asleep, but neither Diana not Roger did. They both felt extremely wide awake. Diana half wished she was going, then changed her mind as she thought of seeing the 'gang', whoever they might be.

'It's almost ten,' whispered Roger to himself. 'I'll wake Snubby. I do hope Loony will be all right without us.'

Snubby sprang up. He whispered goodbye to a most surprised Loony, thrust him into Diana's room and then, while she was making a fuss of him, fled downstairs with the others. They were out in the moonlit garden just as Barney walked out of the shed, and the clock struck ten.

'Good work,' said Barney in a low voice. 'Got your torches? Come on then. Don't put them on though – we can easily see in the moonlight.'

They walked down to Ring O' Bells Hall, and waited while Barney shinned up the ivy and got into the room with the four-poster bed he once slept in. He ran down into the hall and opened the front door to them. They all crept in and shut the door again.

'Let's go into that room over there, and wait,' said Barney. 'I've just remembered, there's a big cupboard there. We could leave the door of the room open, and watch through the crack for the gang to come in – and then pop into the cupboard till they're gone down the secret passage. Then we'll hare up to the police station.'

They went to the room and pushed the door open. Then they got the most terrible shock! There, seated round a candle on a table in the room, were three men and a woman!

The gang must have come early! Run, Barney, run, Roger and Snubby. Run for your very lives!

Chapter Twenty-Five

Headlong into Trouble

Barney and Roger were right in the room before they realised that there was anyone there. Snubby had suddenly paused, seeing a light, and had tried to pull back the others, but they were right in the room by then, and were seen.

The men leapt to their feet at once, staring in astonishment and anger. Roger was petrified, but Barney saw at a glance the danger they were in. He turned to run at once.

'Stop!' shouted one of the men. 'STOP, I say. Who are you? COME HERE!'

In real fear the boys fled out of the room. What a blow! All their wonderful plans were shattered! They would be lucky if they escaped themselves now.

'Separate – hide – quickly!' panted Barney. He darted off towards the kitchen. Snubby fled into a nearby room. Roger made for the little panelled room where the entrance of the secret passage was. The chest! He would hide there.

He felt about in the darkness when he got into the room. Ah – here was the chest! He lifted up the lid and got in. The lid fell with such a noise that he trembled. Surely the men would have heard it.

Snubby didn't at first recognise the room he was in – then as he looked round, panic-stricken, in the moonlight that flooded through a window, he saw that he was in the room that contained the secret chamber up the chimney.

He tore to the fireplace at once, just as he heard the

men outside the room. He pushed himself into the wide chimney, and felt frantically for the steps at the side. Thank goodness, it was the right chimney! He climbed up, and squeezed himself into the dirty, musty, secret cavity.

Only just in time! The three men burst into the room, holding brilliant torches that drowned the silver moonlight. 'He came in here!' cried one. 'I saw him.'

'Then he's here still,' said another man grimly. 'There's only one door – the one he came in by. We'll find him all right!'

Snubby trembled so much that he really wondered if his legs would hold him upright. They didn't! They gave way beneath him and he slid into a sitting position! The men heard the noise he made, sliding down to sit. 'Listen – he's quite near!' said one, and opened the door of a cupboard. It was empty, of course.

'*I* thought the noise came from somewhere over here,' said another man, walking to the fireplace. He poked his head up the enormous chimney and flashed his torch there. Snubby almost groaned. He expected to feel his foot pulled roughly, and to be hauled out.

But the secret chamber was meant to hide people properly, and it did. Not a sign could be seen of the hidden boy in the light of the torch. Only if the man had known of the chamber could he have seen Snubby, by climbing up one of the steps himself. But he didn't know it.

The woman did – but she had gone after Roger! The men hunted all over the room, opened chests and cupboards, looked behind curtains – and finally gave up the search. 'He couldn't have come in here,' they said.

'Lizzie!' called one of them. 'Where are you? Have you found those kids?'

'I've found one of them!' she called back. 'He's in this chest!'

She had heard the banging of the lid and had rushed into the little panelled room. She could see at once that the only hiding-place was in one of the chests. She lifted the lid of the small one. It was empty.

Poor Roger was crouching down in the other, hardly daring to breathe. He heard the lid of his chest lifted, and a torch was flashed in quickly. Then the lid was slammed down immediately – and he heard a key turn in the lock!

Roger clenched his fists. Now he was out of things – locked up well and truly. It was an idiotic thing to do, to let that lid bang down! He could have kicked himself.

The men came into the room and the woman tapped the chest with her torch. 'Here's one anyway,' she said. 'Safe and sound for the moment. What about the other?'

Roger heaved a sigh of relief. So they thought there were only two of them – they couldn't have seen Snubby! Where in the world had he gone? If only he could nip out and go to the police, things would still be all right. But would Snubby be brave enough to do that?

The three men and the woman began a search for Barney. 'Who *are* these kids?' demanded one of the men. 'And what are they doing here at night?'

'They're probably a couple of young hooligans who got in somehow and thought it would be a lark to steal a few things,' said the woman.

'Well – it's just too bad for them, but I'm afraid we shall have to take them off with us tonight and dump them somewhere where they won't be able to split on us for a long, long time,' said one of the men grimly.

'We've *got* to find the other fellow,' said another man. 'Listen – what's that?'

It was Miranda! She was hiding with Barney, not far from the foot of the square tower. He had got behind a great heavy curtain, and was crouching there, his heart beating far too loudly for his liking. Miranda felt that he was scared, and she was scared too.

She didn't like being on a lead when she was frightened. She leapt a little way up the curtain, felt the pull of the lead and fell back again. Barney didn't dare even to whisper to her. She began to gibber a little.

He decided to undo the lead. She might feel happier then. So he slipped the catch and freed her. She was off and away at once. She leapt to the top of a cupboard and ground her teeth in a peculiar way she had when she was both frightened and angry. This was the noise that the men had suddenly heard.

One man flashed his torch in Miranda's direction, and was amazed to see a little monkey there. 'A monkey!' he said. 'The owner must be in this room then. Quick, search everywhere!'

Barney felt concerned. Sooner or later they would come to his curtain. He had no illusions about these men. They were tough and cruel. It would go hardly with any of the boys if they were captured.

He decided to worm his way behind the curtain to where the foot of the tower was. If he could sprint up the steps to the platform, he might find a corner to hide in – some niche the men wouldn't see. It was a forlorn hope but the best he could think of.

The men were on the opposite side of the room, examining every cupboard. Miranda chattered at them angrily, keeping well out of their reach.

Barney came to the end of the curtain. He made a dash for the tower. He rushed safely through the open doorway and sprinted up the stone staircase, round and round and round. Miranda heard him and with a bound she was after him, scuttling up on all fours.

Barney groaned when he saw her. No matter where he

hid up on that little shadowy platform, Miranda would chatter and give him away!

Then a brilliant thought shot into his head – that little room above the bells! He could get up there, and be perfectly safe. He had only to threaten to push down anyone who came up after him! Nobody could ever get him out of there.

He began to climb up the straight wall of the tower, finding the hand and footholds in the stone quite easily, for he had used them once before. Miranda sat chattering angrily on his shoulder. She couldn't understand any of these peculiar happenings at all.

The men raced up the spiral staircase too, with the woman behind. 'You'll get him – there's only a platform at the top – hardly anywhere to hide!' she panted.

But when the first man reached the platform and flashed his torch round, there was no one to see! He shone his torch into one or two shadowy corners – nobody there!

He heard a noise above his head and flashed his torch there in surprise. He was just in time to see Barney's legs disappearing, as the boy clambered through the hole in the roof, from which the bells hung.

'Look there!' he said startled. 'The fellow has actually shinned up this steep wall and climbed through the roof. Can he escape from there?'

'No – unless he squeezes out of the window and flings himself to the ground – where he would certainly be killed,' said the woman. 'We don't need to worry about *him* now! We can shut and lock the big door at the front of the tower, and he'll be as much a prisoner as the other fellow in the chest. Nicely out of our way!'

One man looked doubtfully up at the hole in the ceiling. 'There must be footholds up the wall,' he said. 'I've a good mind to try and shin up myself, and knock the fellow on the head to make sure he doesn't worry us for some time.'

Barney heard all this, of course. He kept well away from the hole, in case one of the men had a revolver. He didn't trust these fellows – he had upset their carefully laid plans, and goodness knew what they would do to him if they had the chance.

He called boldly down. 'I can hear you – and I tell you this – if any of you climb up here, I'll knock him down to the stone platform! I've got the advantage of any of you up here!'

There was a silence. 'He's right,' said one of the men in a low voice. 'He could reach out and strike anyone down, once they got up to the top. Well, we'll do as you say, Lizzie – lock the tower door at the foot, and leave him here to stew!'

'Well, that's the two of them then – and the monkey,' said another man. 'Now let's get about our business. We'd better go down and see our friend. Lizzie says he's pretty bad tonight, so maybe he'll be willing to listen to us.'

Barney heard them go down the spiral staircase. He heard the heavy door at the bottom slam, and he heard the grating sound of the big key being turned in the lock. He sat up in the little room above the bells, gritting his teeth together. All their plans were spoilt! They were prisoners instead of setting someone else free!

'Shall we go down or not, Miranda?' he said. 'Better go down, perhaps, and see if they *really* have locked the door.'

He put his head down to look out of the hole. The bells gleaming in the light of his torch, hung just below him, still and silent. Barney flashed his torch down beside them, trying to see the platform below.

Miranda suddenly gibbered in fright, and clutched at his arm. With all her small monkey strength she tried to pull him back. Barney was surprised. Whatever was the matter?

Chapter Twenty-Six

The Warning of the Bells

'Why are you suddenly so frightened, Miranda?' asked Barney in surprise. 'I'm not going to fall down.'

But still the little monkey gibbered and pulled at him. Barney sat back and looked at her. 'Now what's all this about?' he said. 'Why be in such a state because I put my torch out of the hole?'

He put his torch out again, and by accident it touched one of the bells, which gave out a very small sound – ding!

Miranda went quite mad. She leapt to the window sill as if she were going to go out. Then she leapt back to Barney, squealing pitifully and pulled at him. What *could* be the matter?

'Are you afraid of the bells, Miranda?' asked Barney at last. 'Did they scare you when they rang all by themselves that time? Look – I'll touch them – they won't harm me!'

He stretched out his hand and tapped one of the bells, which said, 'DING' a little more loudly. Miranda scampered into a corner, put her arms across her face, and rocked herself to and fro, moaning as if she were human.

Barney was really nonplussed. He had never seen Miranda like this before. He flashed his torch on the scared, miserable little monkey and pondered. Why? Why? Why?

And then he suddenly knew! Of course! Why ever hadn't he thought of it before?

'Miranda, come here,' he said softly. 'I know why you

are so frightened – you're frightened of the bells, aren't you? Miranda – *you* rang them before, didn't you – when we all thought they had rung themselves? You were up here, exploring – you didn't know what the bells were, or what noise they made – and in your usual inquisitive way you leapt on to them – and set them swinging. And they rang! They jingled and jangled and wouldn't stop!' Miranda still went on moaning to herself. Barney was sad for the little monkey. He went on talking in his quiet, soothing voice.

'You leapt from one to the other in panic, didn't you, Miranda – and you made them ring madly and wildly till you were almost frightened out of your skin. Now you can't bear me even to touch them! Poor little monkey. Come here, Miranda.'

Miranda came, making funny little noises. She cuddled into Barney's arms, comforted by his soft voice, though she couldn't follow what he said.

'There's nothing to be frightened of, Miranda,' said Barney. 'They're only bells. Well, well, well, – so they didn't ring themselves the other night – *you* rang them, though you didn't guess what a noise they would make.'

He sat there with Miranda in his arms, thinking back to the night the bells had rung and frightened them all so much. Then his thoughts slid back to this unfortunate night. They had had high hopes – and now here they were, captured and locked up! He was pretty certain that Roger, anyhow, was captured, and he couldn't imagine Snubby remaining uncaught for long.

Barney thought of the ill man down at the bottom of the secret passage. He thought of the three men and the woman – the 'gang' as the detective had called them. Now they would be able to get out of their unfortunate prisoner all the information they wanted – they would probably leave him there to die – and get away in safety themselves.

How long had they been using this place as their head-quarters? How many plots had they hatched here, how many people had they imprisoned down in the secret passage beyond the brick wall?

Barney wished he knew what was the best thing to do. How could he warn anyone that something was amiss at Ring O' Bells Hall? Was it possible to squeeze out of the window and climb down the ivy, if it grew strongly there?

Then, as he sat there, just above the bells, an idea came to him. Why didn't he think of it before? It was the only thing to do!

He would ring the bells himself! Not as Miranda had rung them, jingle-jangling them in fright – but ring them fiercely and loudly and urgently without stopping! He would rouse the whole of the village! He would bring the police hurrying to the Hall. He would terrify everyone so much that SOMETHING would have to be done!

The another thought struck him. The bells would warn the men too. They might come rushing up, and get away, if they had a car. Barney thought hard. They would now be down in the secret passage, far below the foundations of the house – beyond the brick wall, which must have a way through it somehow. They couldn't possibly hear the bells there!

'The bells will warn the whole village – but not the men.' Barney decided exultantly. 'It's an idea – a wonderful idea. Miranda, darling, I'm going to give you the fright of your life, I'm afraid – but it can't be helped. I'm going to ring the bells!'

Barney lay down flat on the floor of the little tower room. He leaned out of the hole, and stretched his arms down to the short ropes on which the bells were tightly hung. He caught hold of them.

He rang the bells. How he rang them! Surely never,

never before had those bells rung so wildly, so madly, so insistently.

'Jingle, Jangle-jangle, jing, jing, JING, jangle, JANG, JANG, jingle, jing, JING, JANG, JING, JANG, JING, JANG. . . .'

The noise up in the little tower was terrific. Miranda gave a loud howl and bounded to the window. She was out of it in a trice. Barney didn't notice. His head was down through the hole, and he was pulling the short ropes for all he was worth, panting hard.

Roger, down in the chest, heard them, and was terrified. The bells! Ringing by themselves again! They must know that enemies were here, right in the very house. He crouched down in the locked chest, trembling, wondering if the men could hear them too.

Snubby heard them, half-standing, half-sitting in the secret cavity of the old fireplace. He was in a most uncomfortable position. When he heard the tremendous loud noise of the bells, breaking the silence so suddenly and urgently, he almost fell out of the secret chamber. He sank down till he was sitting flat again. He shook so much that even his teeth rattled in his head.

'The bells!' he thought to himself. 'The bells again! How do they know? How do they guess that enemies are here?'

Neither he nor Roger imagined that it was Barney who was ringing them. They didn't even know that Barney was up in the tower.

Snubby was far too frightened to move out of his hiding-place. For all he knew the men might be waiting somewhere to pounce on him. He was quite, quite determined not to stir from the secret chamber. How well he knew now what fugitives had felt when they crammed themselves into this little secret hidey-hole. Now that he heard the bells ringing, he was all the more certain that nothing,

166

nothing, nothing would make him leave the chimney-place!

The men and the woman down below in the secret passage heard almost nothing of the bells. The place where they were now, beyond the brick wall, was sound-proof to the jangle of the bells so high up in the tower. All they heard was a slightly tinny noise from somewhere which didn't make them suspect any danger at all.

But the sound of the bells went far and wide over the countryside. The jangling leapt out of the old tower and penetrated into cottage windows, and into dog kennels, and into the barns. This was no hurried, flurried spell of ringing such as the bells had given before—it was a sum-mons, a warning, a signal of danger!

Dogs barked. Cows lowed. Cats fled to corners. Men threw the bedclothes off and leapt out of bed. Women screamed. Miss Hannah and Miss Pepper awoke in a hurry.

Diana comforted the amazed Loony, while Loopy put himself in a cupboard.

Diana was frightened. Those bells again! What was happening down at the Hall? Were the boys all right?

The two policemen at the police station, dozing in their chairs, sprang up, astonished, at the sound of the bells. One reached at once for his helmet.

'Something's up!' he said. 'Where's Joe? Tell him to phone through to Lillinghame, just in case we need their help. 'Something's up! Just listen to those bells!'

Down towards Ring O' Bells Hall went a crowd of scared, wondering villagers. Some of the men had pitch-forks, some had sticks. Why did they bring them? They didn't know! Something was up, at the Hall—and till they knew what it was they were taking no chances.

The police joined them on bicycles. 'What's to do?' the villagers shouted to them. 'Who's ringing the bells?'

But the police knew no more than anyone else!

They came to the Hall. It was in complete darkness. Not a light was to be seen in any room. But still the bells clashed out urgently.

'Someone must be in the tower, surely!' cried a man.

'The bells ring themselves,' said an old man somberly. 'Always did!'

'Here's a car!' cried a woman, shining a torch on to a big car shoved right up against the hedge, not far from Ring O' Bells Hall.

'Ha!' said one of the policemen. 'Here – where's Joe! Joe, you take charge of this car. Take out the key, to start with. Now then, where's Bill? Oh, there you are – we're going to get into Ring O' Bells Hall, if we have to break the door down!'

The police hammered at the great front door of the Hall. Barney couldn't hear the noise, up in the tower room, but Roger, hidden in the chest, heard it, and Snubby, trembling violently up the chimney, heard it too. He felt sick. Now what was up?

He heard a stentorian voice outside the front door.

'OPEN IN THE NAME OF THE LAW!'

But the front door, of course, did not open. It trembled under the hammering the policeman was giving it, but it remained firm. The policeman tried again.

'OPEN IN THE NAME OF THE LAW!'

'It's the police,' thought Snubby, and was flooded with relief. 'The police! They heard the bells and they've come! I'll open the door to them. Oh, WHAT a relief!'

Chapter Twenty-Seven

Plenty of Excitement

Snubby forgot his fears. He scrambled down from the secret chamber, almost falling headlong into the great fireplace. He rushed across the room, out of the door and into the hall. Very little moonlight entered there, and it looked very dark. But Snubby was feeling extraordinarily brave now.

He ran to the front door, tripping over a mat or two. He turned the great handle and swung the door back.

The police had powerful torches, and they flashed them on to Snubby at once, not quite knowing what to expect. They gaped when they saw a sooty-faced boy of about twelve, grinning joyfully at them!

'Here – what's all this?' said the first policeman. 'What are you doing here? And who's ringing those bells?'

'I don't know,' said Snubby. 'Gosh, I'm glad you came. Those bells are ringing to say that enemies are here. Look out, won't you!'

The villagers began to crowd in too. The policeman swung round. 'Where's Joe? Joe, keep these people back. May be danger here for all we know.'

The bells went on ringing madly. Barney was doing the thing properly! He had rests every now and again, but he made up his mind to go on ringing them till something happened.

The two policemen went to the foot of the square tower. They meant to find out who was ringing the bells. Snubby followed some way behind. He was quite certain they were ringing themselves, and he didn't particularly want to go near bells that behaved in such a strange manner.

The police unlocked the door at the foot of the tower. They went up the spiral staircase cautiously, torches in hand. They came out on to the platform. Barney saw the light of their torches immediately, and withdrew his hands from the bell-ropes. He looked down warily. Who was this – enemy or friend?

To his great relief, he saw the dark-blue uniform of the police. He almost fell down the hole with joy. The bells gradually stopped jangling, and the first policeman called up in a stern and commanding voice.

'You up there! What do you think you're doing, ringing bells in the dead of night? Who are you?'

'Wait a moment and I'll come down and tell you,' called Barney. He slipped through the hole, held the guide-rope, found the first footholds and climbed down the tower wall like a cat. The police watched him in astonishment. He leapt down beside them.

'Another boy!' said the first policeman. 'Now you just tell me what all this is about, young fellow!'

'It's serious,' said Barney. 'Very serious. Did you ever hear of someone called Detective Inspector Rawlings?'

This unexpected question made both the policemen gape in surprise. 'What do you know about *him*?' rapped out the first one.

'I'll tell you,' said Barney, and tried to tell his extraordinary story as shortly as possible. It took the policemen some time to grasp what he was trying to tell them.

'Secret passages – Rawlings behind a brick wall down there – ill, perhaps dying – the gang here tonight – who *are* they, anyway? And where are they? Tell us, boy, quick!'

'I'm trying to tell you,' said Barney impatiently. 'But what you don't realise is that it's all very urgent. The men are down there *now* with Rawlings. You can catch them and rescue him, if you're quick! That's what he planned for you to do, with our help. But things went wrong, so I rang the bells to get somebody here.'

At last it dawned on the policemen that things really were urgent. They went down the spiral staircase, almost falling over Snubby, who was half-way up listening to what Barney was saying, with very great interest. So it was old Barney who had done all that bell-ringing! Gosh!

'Hallo, Snubby – where's Roger?' called Barney, catching sight of Snubby.

'No idea,' said Snubby.

'Who's Roger? Another of you?' asked the policeman, marvelling at coming across so many boys in the middle of the night.

'He's my cousin,' said Snubby. 'When we were chased, we all separated and hid. I don't know where Roger hid.'

'I'll take you to the entrance of the secret passage,' said Barney, and he guided the two policemen to the little panelled room. 'The passage begins here,' said Barney. 'I'll just – '

But he was interrupted by a terrible noise in the chest nearby. Roger had heard Barney's voice and was clamouring to be let out! He knocked with his heels on the floor of the chest, hammered with his fists and yelled at the top of his voice. 'Let me out! I'm here. Let me out!'

'Bless us all!' said the policeman, startled. 'What's that now? Who's in there? Is this a pantomime, or what?'

'It's Roger,' said Barney thankfully, and he unlocked the chest. Roger sprang up like a jack-in-the-box. 'What's happened?' he cried. 'I heard the bells.'

'Tell you later, Roger,' said Barney. 'Look, did you hear the gang go down into the passage?'

'Yes,' said Roger, 'the three men and the woman.'

'Have they come back yet?'

'No,' said Roger. 'I thought they might when I heard the bells. But they shut the secret panel, and I reckon the noise of the bells didn't reach them enough to scare them. The tower is a good way away from here. I heard them, of course.'

'Where's the secret panel?' said the first policeman. Barney showed him how to slide it back. He was most astonished.

'Such goings on!' he muttered, and was about to stick his head into the hole, when Barney pulled him back.

'Wait – they're coming back. I can hear them. Better be careful, they're tough.'

Sure enough, the sound of voices and footsteps could now be heard. Silently Barney slid the panel into place again, and they all stood waiting. Could they catch the whole gang – or would the first one give warning so that the others would run back?

A most unfortunate thing happened. The second policeman felt a sneeze coming. It was a large sneeze, he knew that. He groped for his handkerchief, feeling as if he were going to burst – which is practically what he did do, when the sneeze came. It was quite colossal, and almost blew Snubby to one side. He jumped violently.

The first policeman gave an angry mutter, then everything was silent again. There was now no noise from behind the passage. The 'gang' had evidently heard the explosion and had stopped to consider the matter.

The men apparently eventually decided that the woman had better go and investigate. Soft footsteps came up to the closed secret panel. In a moment or two it slid quietly back a crack, and the woman shone a torch through the crack.

When she saw the silent group in the room she shut the panel with a scream, and called back to the men. 'It's the police! They're here!'

She stumbled back in panic. The first policeman slid back the panel with a bang and shouted down the passage. 'You come on here, and give yourselves up. You're cornered. It'll be the worse for you if you don't come now.'

A loud and sarcastic laugh came up the passage. 'Sez you! Come and get us! Anybody coming down this passage will be neatly picked off!'

That made the policeman hesitate quite a bit. He considered things for a moment and then called down again.

'Bring Detective Inspector Rawlings up here at once.'

'Sez you!' said the mocking voice again. 'He'll be a nice little hostage now, won't he? He's ill, you know, and he needs a doctor badly. We'll give you your inspector if you let us go. Otherwise – well I doubt if he'll last till the morning!'

As if to underline what they said, a terrible rasping cough came up the passage way, muffled by distance, but still dreadful to hear.

'He *is* very ill, sir,' whispered Barney.

'Well – what are we to do?' said the policeman, exasperated. 'No one can go down there without being in grave danger, that's certain. If only we knew of another way to out-flank them.'

'I know another way, sir,' whispered Barney. 'This secret passage runs a long way – up to an old woman's cottage – it comes out half-way down her well.'

The policeman began to think he must be dreaming. 'Where's Joe?' he said, turning round. 'Joe, stay here and see no one escapes this way. You've got your truncheon, haven't you? You know what to do. I'm going with this boy.'

Leaving the useful Joe behind, the two policemen followed Barney, Snubby and Roger to the front door, where an excited crowd of people were still waiting.

'You can go home,' said the first policeman gruffly.

173

'You'll be told the news tomorrow. Can't tell you any-thing. Here you, Jim – go and telephone to Lillinghame and tell them we do want them, and the quicker the better.'

'We'd better wait till they come, I think, sir,' said Barney. 'This gang is pretty desperate, according to Detective Inspector Rawlings. I've got a plan, if you'd like to hear it.'

'Come back into the Hall then, and we'll listen,' said the policeman. He and his companion, and the three boys went into a nearby room. The policeman sat down and turned to Barney. 'Go ahead,' he said.

'Well, sir,' said Barney. 'We know another way into the secret passage, which leads to where the inspector is lying. There are two roof-falls which we shall have to deal with. He is just behind the bigger of the two. Now, what I propose is this – '

He paused, thinking. 'Go on, then,' said the policeman, and Snubby and Roger bent forward, wondering what plan Barney had thought of.

'These men won't know we're coming from the opposite direction,' said Barney. 'They won't be expecting that. They'll just be keeping guard on the other end of the passage – so, if we surprise them from the opposite end, we'll capture the lot!'

Chapter Twenty-Eight

A Very Nice Evening's Work!

'Pah!' said the policeman. 'They'll hear us coming.'

'I'd thought of that,' said Barney. 'Could you arrange with Joe or somebody to create a disturbance up this end, so that all the gang would think they were going to be rushed, and would have their attention on this secret passage here – '

'And not be watching the other end!' cried Roger. 'So that we could break in there and take them from the rear. Good work, Barney!'

'Ah I see,' said the policeman. 'Yes – quite a good idea. But how shall we make sure that there's a disturbance this end at the same time as we want to break through?'

'Easy,' said Barney. 'Set a definite time, sir – and we'll count on the disturbance being set in motion here at that time, we'll know the gang will be guarding the secret passage here, and we'll be able to break through behind them nicely!'

'Yes – it sounds all right,' said the policeman. 'What time shall we say?'

'Let me see – it'll take a little time to get to Ring O' Bells Cottage,' said Barney, calculating. 'And then down the well, and along the tunnel – remove the roof falls, or it will be difficult for all of us to get through. I should think if you said in two hours' time, sir, that would be about right.'

'Good – say three o'clock then,' said the policeman, consulting his watch. 'All these goings on in the middle of the night! Where's Joe? He'd better be told about this, and told to set his watch by ours.'

'I'll tell him,' said Roger, and went off to the useful and very solid-looking Joe. He promised to create a terrific diversion at exactly three o'clock.

'Shouting and hammering and such-like?' he said. 'Yes, I can do that all right. I'll have some of the Lillinghame fellows with me, too, by then.'

The Lillinghame men arrived in another two minutes. There were four of them.

'Where's Joe?' said the Ring O' Bells policeman. 'I want two of you Lillinghame fellows to stay with him. He'll tell you what's up. And I want you other two to come with me. I'll tell you the tale as we go. We mustn't hang about here any longer.'

They set off with the three boys. Barney had suggested taking a couple of spades, and these were borrowed from one of the villagers.

As they were going along the road, a little dark shape dropped down from a tree on to Barney's shoulder. 'Miranda,' he said thankfully. 'So you've come back. I was so worried about you. I knew you were terribly scared.'

'Who's Miranda now?' asked the first policeman, feeling that he couldn't cope with much more. He shone his torch on her and gave a jump. 'A monkey? What next? Is she coming with us too?'

'She is,' said Barney cheerfully. 'I'm not losing her again tonight! She nearly went off her head when she heard those bells!'

They walked quietly through the wood to Naomi's cottage. There was no light in her windows. She was in bed and fast asleep.

'To the well, sir,' said Barney in a low voice. He lowered himself over the side and went quickly down, holding on to the iron loops that stuck out from the brickwork.

The first policeman stared in horror, flashing his torch down.

'Here – what's all this? Surely we haven't got to go down here? Why, it's a very deep well!'

'It's quite safe,' said Roger, and he went down too, followed by Snubby, who was now almost speechless with excitement. What *would* the boys at school say to all this?

The police followed very reluctantly. The two spades were let down on string. At last everyone was safely through the hole in the side of the well, and started on their way through the secret tunnel.

Nobody liked it much, though the three boys didn't find it quite as strange as the policemen because they had been that way before.

The spades came in useful at the first roof fall, which was soon tackled so that everyone could go through easily. As they came near the second one, Barney stood still and warned the policeman behind him.

'We're almost there. What's the time, sir? It's not three o'clock yet, is it?'

'Five minutes more,' said the policeman.

'Well, we'd better get as close to the second roof fall as we can – the inspector is lying just behind that – and wait for three o'clock. We may hear something of the commotion above. We may not, of course, but we shall at least hear some exclamation from the men, and possibly hear them leaving the place where the inspector is and going through the brick wall.'

'How do they get through that?' inquired the policeman, feeling rather dazed.

'I don't know, sir – I guess they can take out enough loose bricks to get through all right,' said Barney. 'Now, we'd better move on, sir. It must be almost three.'

They moved silently up to the second roof fall. The crack through which Barney had seen the sick man had disappeared. The rubble had shifted a little and covered it.

The dreadful cough came rasping through the roof fall to the ears of the waiting company. 'He sounds very ill,' whispered the policeman uncomfortably. 'Poor chap. We must get him off to hospital at once.'

There were muffled voices to be heard behind the roof fall. Then, in the far-off distance, came echoes of some kind of noise. The men on the other side of the roof fall started up at once.

'What's that!' said one of them, in a loud voice. 'They're coming! Quick, up the passage! Got your gun, Charlie? We'll soon show them we mean business!'

There was silence after that, except for the distant noises that kept echoing through to the watchers by the roof fall. They came from the valiant Joe and his helpers, no doubt, making their 'commotion!'

'Quick, sir – where are the spades? Let's got through now,' said Barney urgently. Soon the spades were at work on the rubble, and in no time at all a way was cleared through. Beyond was a small, widened-out chamber in the tunnel, with a rough bed, a bench, candles, and a jug of water. On the couch lay a man, breathing heavily.

'Inspector Rawlings!' said the first policeman. 'We're here!'

The ill man turned bloodshot eyes to the company crowding into the little chamber. He smiled feebly. 'Good,' he said, 'good. Get them, Brown. They're tough, so look out. Keep those boys back, though.'

He began to cough again. Silently the policemen crossed to the brick wall that enclosed the other side of the little hidden room. There was an opening there big enough for a man to get through.

Barney had a look at it. Yes – it was as he had expected. Certain bricks were loose and could be easily removed.

He was about to follow the last policeman with Roger and Snubby when he was pushed back.

'No kids in this,' said the policeman's voice, rough but kindly.

'I'm not a kid,' said Barney indignantly.

'You're to keep out of this,' said the policeman. 'You'll only cramp our style. Do as you're told, youngster.'

Barney knew when orders had to be obeyed. He sat down beside the man on the couch, who had now closed his eyes and seemed to be in an uneasy sleep. He breathed so loudly and with such difficulty that it was painful to hear him.

'We're out of the most exciting part of all,' said Snubby gloomily.

'You wouldn't like it a bit if you were in it,' said Roger. 'I wonder what's happening. Hark!'

There was suddenly a loud disturbance up the passage, shouting, yelling, and the woman was squealing. It went on for some time, and then a policeman came grinning down to the secret room. He stuck his red face through the hole in the brickwork.

'All finished!' he said. 'They were waiting for Joe and the others to attack from above – and we crept up behind and were on them before they could even turn round. They never heard us at all. I'm not surprised, with the din old Joe was making.'

'Are they all caught?' asked Barney in delight.

'Yes – and we've got the woman too – Lizzie the Go-Between,' said the policeman. 'We've been after her for a long time – and here she was at Ring O' Bells under our very noses. Come on up. We're sending a doctor down here now, and the poor old inspector will have to be taken up above and put into hospital. He's in a bad way.'

'I'm all right,' said a weak voice, and the ill man opened

his eyes. 'I feel a lot better now I know the gang is arrested. I know a lot about them, and a lot about their friends. I – '

He began to cough. 'Now don't you say a word, Inspector,' said the policeman kindly. 'Don will soon be here.'

He beckoned to the boys, and they climbed through the hole in the brickwork. The policeman then climbed into the little hidden room, to stay with the inspector till help came.

Up the passage went the boys, and behind the secret panelling. A helmeted head was poking inside the open hole in the panelling. 'Oh, it's you boys,' said the head. 'Come on, now.'

The boys climbed out. There seemed to be quite a crowd of people in the little panelled room – any amount of policemen, the woman, the three men belonging to the gang, and a man they saw was a doctor. He disappeared into the secret passage at once, carrying a small black bag.

The three men and the woman were handcuffed. They all looked angry and sullen and the woman looked scared. She was astonished when she saw the boys. She recognised them at once.

'You!' she said, hissing at them. 'So it was *you*, prying and snooping and – '

'Shut up,' said one of the gang sharply. The woman subsided, but she glared all the time at the boys as if she would like to bite them.

'A very nice evening's work,' said one of the men from Lillinghame, who seemed to be an inspector, and very much in charge of the proceedings now. 'A nice little haul – and a prospect of further hauls, when we get some information from Inspector Rawlings!'

'You go home now, you kids,' said the policeman who had directed proceedings in the tunnel. 'We'll see you tomorrow. You've done well. Now go home and sleep – if you can!'

Chapter Twenty-Nine

All Good Things End!

It was all very well to say: 'Go home and sleep.' For one thing there really wasn't very much of the night left, and for another thing, who in the world could go to bed and sleep peacefully after such an adventurous night?

Feeling very much awake and on top of the world the three boys left the Hall and went up the road once more. Miranda was on Barney's shoulder, rather subdued by all the queer happenings of the night.

'She'll never like bells again,' said Barney, fondling her. 'Will you, Miranda? She must have made for the window in the tower, and vanished out of it.'

'Diana will be wondering what's been happening,' said Roger. 'I'm surprised she and Miss Pepper and Miss Hannah didn't come down to see what the matter was.'

There were lights in the front room, when the boys arrived. Diana was looking out for them anxiously, with a worried and angry Loony by her side. The spaniel hurled himself on Snubby like a cannonball as soon as he came into the hall, and Loopy followed suit. For a few minutes nobody could make themselves heard through the excited barking.

'Boys! What *has* been happening? How *could* you go off like that without telling us?' cried Miss Pepper. 'Diana told me such a peculiar tale that I could hardly believe it. What *is* all this about secret passages and bells and a sick man and – '

'We can tell you everything now, Miss Pepper,' said Roger, grinning. He looked pale and tired but very cheerful. Barney looked the same as usual. Snubby looked incredibly dirty, through having stayed so long in the secret chimney cavity. Miranda was not to be seen. She was curled up inside Barney's shirt, and not even a paw was showing. Miranda was too tired for words!

Bit by bit the strange story came out. Miss Hannah's eyes nearly dropped out of her head. 'Such goings on!' she said. 'I never heard such things in my life.'

Barney explained about the bells, and how he had rung them to awaken the village and perhaps startle the police, and how marvellously his plan had worked.

'The bells woke *us* up,' said Miss Pepper. 'I was really scared. I couldn't help remembering the old legend. I couldn't imagine there was anyone in the tower at that time of night, ringing the bells – and fancy its being *you*, Barney!'

'Gosh, I did ring them hard,' said Barney. 'They absolutely deafened me. I had to ring them by their short little ropes, you see, so I was almost touching them. I'm certain sure it was Miranda who rang them the first time – by accident, I expect. She probably jumped down on to them without knowing they would jangle, then got terrified and did a lot more jumping.'

'Poor Miranda,' said Snubby, and put his hand inside Barney's shirt to feel the warm little bundle. Miranda didn't stir.

Miss Hannah had got some cake and milk and they all ate as they talked. 'Funny how hungry an adventure makes you,' said Snubby. 'I haven't felt hungry like this for ages.'

'Fibber,' said Diana. 'You're always saying that. Goodness, Snubby, I did have an awful time here all alone, wondering and wondering what was happening to you. I simply couldn't bear it – and Loony was a frightful nuisance. I had to hold his nose into the cushion when he began howling in case Miss Pepper heard him.'

'Woof,' said Loony mournfully, looking reproachfully at Snubby.

'It's dawn,' said Diana, looking out of the window. 'The sun will soon be up. I shouldn't think it's worth while going to bed, is it, Miss Pepper?'

'Certainly it is,' said Miss Pepper, who was feeling rather dazed with all she had be told. These children! It was really *dangerous* to look after them. You simply never knew what they would do next.

She got up. 'Come along,' she said. 'Get into bed just as you are, dirt and all! Just slip into your pyjamas and crawl in. Sleep till twelve o'clock if you like.'

'Good gracious – we'll be awake *long* before then!' said Snubby, and got up, yawning loudly.

They were not awake long before then. They all slept till past eleven o'clock, and they would not have awakened then if Loopy hadn't given such a fusillade of barks that they all sat up with a jump. Snubby rose to the window and looked to see why Loopy was barking so madly.

'It's the police!' he said excitedly. 'Three of them – all looking very important. Come on – get dressed and come down.'

'You'd better wash your face, Snubby,' said Roger. 'Hey, Barney, stir yourself a bit more!'

Barney had actually been allowed to sleep on a couch in Roger's room, with Miranda tucked into his arms. Miss Hannah couldn't bear to send him out into the shed, and most heroically said that Miranda could sleep on the couch too.

Soon they were all downstairs, and the police welcomed them with broad smiles.

'What have you come for?' asked Snubby eagerly.

'Oh, just to see if we could persuade you three boys to join the police force,' said the inspector smiling. 'I feel you'd be a real help.'

Snubby really believed this. He gazed exultantly at the inspector. 'Gosh – not go back to school, do you mean?'

'Fathead,' said Roger, and gave him a poke in the ribs. 'Don't you know a joke when you hear one?'

'Oh,' said Snubby, and looked so bitterly disappointed that the three policemen guffawed with laughter.

'We came to clear up a few points,' said the inspector. 'How did you come to guess there was any funny business going on at the Hall?'

Barney told them how a man had given him a lift, dropped him at Lillinghame – and then, to his surprise, he had seen him again at the Hall that night.

'I know it was him – he had the same van, with "PIG-GOTT, ELECTRICIAN" on the side,' said Barney. The policemen looked at one another and nodded.

'Just what we wanted to know,' said the inspector, and wrote it down. 'We've had our eye on Piggott for some time. He's always making peculiar little trips to the Bristol Channel and round about here. Now we know why. When his pals come up to the Channel with one or two men on board who want to get into the country and keep hidden till they've got papers, Piggott is at hand. And when a little kidnapping is done, Piggott is again at hand with his van. It probably has a false bottom. We'll examine it carefully.'

'To think that such things go on!' said poor Miss Hannah, who really was upset at all these sudden happenings.

'Another thing we want to clear up,' said the inspector, 'is about the bells ringing the first time. Who rang them then?'

'Miranda, my monkey, I think,' said Barney.

'Were you in the Hall with her?' asked the inspector. 'I understand it was at night.'

'Yes, sir,' said Barney, looking very uncomfortable. 'I'd nowhere to sleep, so I shinned up the ivy and slept in a four-poster bed there. I suppose I did wrong, sir.'

'You did,' said the inspector. 'But I understand you're a circus lad, without a home – you sleep anywhere you can.'

'That's right, sir,' said Barney. 'I hope you won't hold it against me, sir. I didn't do any harm.'

'It won't even be reported,' said the inspector. 'You're a good lad and a brave one. Have you anywhere to sleep now?'

'Yes,' said Miss Hannah surprisingly. 'He's going to stay here with me until the other children leave in about a week's time. I'll look after him.'

Barney looked at her in grateful surprise. Diana gave Miss Hannah a sudden hug, and Snubby yelled 'Hurrah!' Roger rubbed his hands joyfully. Now they would all be together properly. Good old Miss Hannah!

'Well – if he's under your care, he'll be all right,' said the inspector, with a twinkle. 'There won't be any more borrowing of four-poster beds – or, er – tablecloths! We noticed how creased and crumpled they were when we found the four-poster bed had been slept in – and that couch downstairs.'

'Barney's all right,' said Snubby loyally. 'You can always trust old Barney, sir.'

'I think I agree with you,' said the inspector, giving Barney a little nod. He asked a few more questions and then shut his notebook. 'That's all,' he said. 'And I wish you a very happy week – without even the *smell* of an adventure to spoil it!'

'Oh, sir,' protested Snubby. 'Adventures don't spoil things. I say – could we go to the Hall today, and get down that secret passage again – we didn't really examine the hole in the brick wall properly, or the secret room beyond. Did you see that little cupboard, sir, with the candles and things?'

'Oh, yes,' said the inspector. 'We probably saw as much as you did, though not quite so soon. Those candles were kept there, I imagine, to light the secret room when it was occupied. You can certainly go down to the Hall if you wish, and explore anything you like – on one condition.'

'What's that?' asked Roger.

'That you will ring the bells at once if you find any prisoner, crook or suspicious person hiding in any secret cavity, chamber, passage or room,' said the inspector solemnly.

'Good gracious,' said Miss Hannah, half-alarmed. The children laughed.

'We promise!' they said, and took the three policemen to the front gate. The children watched them go ponderously down the road, while they stood there talking. Loony and Loopy got tired of it and ran off.

Presently Miss Hannah called to them. 'Are you coming in to brunch?' The children turned in surprise.

'Brunch?' said Diana doubtfully. 'What's that?'

'Just a mixture of breakfast and lunch,' called back Miss Hannah cheerfully. 'It's nearly twelve o'clock, you know – too late for breakfast, too early for lunch – so you'll have to make do with brunch.'

Brunch proved to be a really wonderful meal, beginning with bacon and eggs, going on to tongue and salad and finishing up with tinned pineapple and cream. Snubby approved highly.

'Why don't we always have brunch?' he said. 'I say, Barney – Miranda's helped herself to a handful of pine-

187

apple chunks. Greedy thing – I was going to have a second helping!'

Miranda sat nibbling her juicy pineapple chunks, her bright monkey eyes keeping watch on Snubby, as if she were afraid he might snatch them from her. Loony put his head on Snubby's knee. Loopy immediately put his head on Snubby's other knee.

Snubby sighed happily. 'Gosh – another whole week of brunches and rides and games with Loony and Loopy and Miranda, and Barney living with us here – it's too good to be true.'

'Woof,' agreed Loony, licking Snubby's bare knee. Loopy at once licked the other one.

'Well,' said Barney, reaching for his glass of lemonade, 'good luck, everyone – and here's to our Next Adventure!'

Stories of Mystery and Adventure by Enid Blyton
in Armada

Mystery Series

Secrets Series

ARMADA

Enid Blyton
Five Find-Outers
Mystery Stories
in Armada

ARMADA

Enid Blyton
School Stories

Have you read all the stories in these great Enid Blyton series:

St Clare's

The Twins at St Clare's	£2.99	☐
The O'Sullivan Twins	£2.99	☐
Summer Term at St Clare's	£2.99	☐
Second Form at St Clare's	£2.99	☐
Claudine at St Clare's	£2.99	☐
Fifth Formers at St Clare's	£2.99	☐

Malory Towers

First Term at Malory Towers	£2.99	☐
Second Form at Malory Towers	£2.99	☐
Third Year at Malory Towers	£2.99	☐
Upper Fourth at Malory Towers	£2.99	☐
In the Fifth at Malory Towers	£2.99	☐
Last Term at Malory Towers	£2.99	☐

ORDER FORM

To order direct from the publishers, just make a list of the titles you want and fill in the form below:

Name_____

Address_____
_____

_____

Send to: Dept 6, HarperCollins Publishers Ltd, Westerhill Road, Bishopbriggs, Glasgow G64 2QT.

Please enclose a cheque or postal order to the value of the cover price, plus:

UK & BFPO: Add £1.00 for the first book, and 25p per copy for each addition book ordered.

Overseas and Eire: Add £2.95 service charge. Books will be sent by surface mail but quotes for airmail despatch will be given on request.

A 24-hour telephone ordering service is available to Visa and Access card holders:
041-772 2281